Bangles *and* Broken Hearts

Bangles *and* Broken Hearts

A Tale of Sticky Situations, Lust, and Heartbreak

TAMIA GORE-FELTON

ISBN: 978-1-4834-3431-5 (sc)
ISBN: 978-1-4834-3430-8 (e)

Library of Congress Control Number: 2015910649

Lulu Publishing Services rev. date: 7/15/2015

To my nearest and dearest. Thanks for your motivation and words of encouragement.

1

Life in the Fast Lane

I couldn't believe that Melody and I were finally nineteen. Mom threw us a surprise party on a chilly Sunday afternoon. The food was on point—barbecue chicken, ribs, hot dogs, hamburgers, and all of the fixings. A few of our friends showed up to celebrate with us. Mom even hired a deejay to play a few of our favorite tunes.

We all laughed and danced to the Electric Slide as the party came to an end. Everyone who was there pitched in with the cleaning. I put away all of the food and fixed take-out plates. Melody collected all of the soda cans and water bottles for some recycling thing her class was doing.

After everyone left, Melody took a shower and prepared her things for school the next day. I, on the other hand, was waiting for Mom to go to sleep. I wanted to slip out and see one of my sugar daddies. By nine thirty both Mom and Melody were asleep. I quietly took the car keys from the hook and drove across town to Jerry's place.

The mood was set when I got there. Jerry smothered me with kisses and gave me my birthday present as soon as I got in the door. I unwrapped the box to find a 14 karat gold bangle. After adding it to the growing collection of bangles on my arm, I thanked Jerry. As I started to stuff the empty box into my purse, Jerry said, "There's something else in the box, Lyric." I then noticed something green in the bottom. It was a one-hundred-dollar bill. I retrieved the crisp bill and put the box and money in my purse.

After putting the evidence away, I hugged Jerry. His hands maneuvered under my shirt until he successfully unfastened my bra and led me into his bedroom. After ten full minutes of huffing and puffing, Jerry was done. I wasn't fully satisfied, but he was, and that was all that mattered. I had to keep him happy in order to keep myself happy. That was the only way he would continue to shower me with gifts and cash.

On the way back home from Jerry's house I breathed a huge sigh of relief. His wife had almost caught us in the act again. I hid in his closet until his wife went down to the basement to check on the laundry she had started before work. As soon as I heard the basement stairs creaking, I made a mad dash for the back door. I then power-walked two and a half blocks, jumped in the car I shared with my sister, and drove away. This was the second time some crap like this had happened. Next time Jerry was going to have to get us a room at an hourly rate.

When I reached my neighborhood, I cut the headlights because I had broken curfew once again. Mom was going to hang me out to dry if she caught me. The bangles on my left arm clinked as I inserted the key into the doorknob. I quickly quieted them as I entered the house. Immediately, I heard the television blasting. This normally got under my skin, but tonight I was thankful someone had left it on so loud. I crept up the stairs quickly. When I reached my room, I peeled off my clothes and glanced at the clock. It was almost two o'clock in the morning. I had only about five hours to sleep until my alarm was due to go off.

I was jerked out of my REM stage of sleep when I heard police-type knocking on my locked bedroom door. Shit! I had slept through my alarm. I instantly jumped up and unlocked the door with my sheet dragging behind me like a train on a wedding dress. My mom screamed from down the hallway, "Lyric, if you don't get your ass up, you're going to be late for school and I'm tired of you locking that damn door!"

I groggily replied, "I'm up, Mom. I'm up."

With that said the fussing began. "Lyric, why can't you be up and on time like your sister? She's downstairs waiting for you like always."

I replied, "Mom, please don't start. I don't feel like hearing that this morning. Give me a minute. You know I'm not a morning person." I then yelled with all of the attitude I could muster, "Why are you always comparing me to Melody? I know that we are twins and everything, but we are still two totally different people."

I didn't get a response out of Mom. I guessed she had decided to leave me alone. I was glad because we went through this just about every morning: the banging on my bedroom door, the fussing, and then the ignoring me when I started to fuss back. Nineteen years of this, and you would think she would get tired of reciting the same old stuff, Monday through Friday. Nope, not my mom. Just as I was about to turn on my radio, Mom yelled from downstairs, "You're not the one who has a job, and you can't even get your lazy behind out of bed on time. Lyric, what am I going to do with you?"

I said under my breath, "Leave me the hell alone, hopefully."

When the yelling match was over, I sat on the edge of my disheveled bed and bit my nails. Mom had my nerves already frazzled this morning. I was so tired of her and everyone else comparing me to Melody. Mom always put her up on a pedestal, but it was nothing new to me. I was used to it. It all had started the night I was born.

Melody and I are identical twins, but we were born in different years and on different days. I was born December 31, 1989, at 11:58 p.m. Melody was born on January 1, 1990, at 12:05 a.m. I had Mom and Dad's full attention for a whopping seven minutes before my competition was brought into this world. My family called me the eighties baby and Melody the nineties newbie until we were about seven.

That was about the same time that Melody and I got a crazy case of chicken pox and missed over two months of school. Even though our absences were excused, Mom and Dad decided to hold us back. They feared that we had fallen behind with the curriculum and didn't want us to suffer in the second grade. That's why my sister and I were now nineteen in the twelfth grade.

For as long as I could remember, I had always been the backup child compared to Melody. I kept to myself and watched as Melody excelled at swimming, gymnastics, and piano. No matter what I did, Melody always managed to outshine me. So I stopped being involved, both with family and with recreational activities. If the family went out to celebrate anything for Melody, I stayed home, as long as Mom didn't make me go. I didn't care that she won writing awards, won medals for track, and was voted most likely to succeed. I wished someone would give me a pat on the back sometimes. Didn't anybody notice that I made some grape Kool-Aid yesterday and didn't leave the jug empty in the fridge like I normally do?

Thinking about the Kool-Aid reminded me of the time I made some special punch for the family. While they were out celebrating one of Melody's many achievements, I acted like I had bad period cramps so I wouldn't have to go with them. This wasn't a total lie. I was sick—sick of about a hundred different things that all had to do with me being compared to Melody. Most of all, I was tired of being called the eighties baby, and I finally decided to do something about it.

As soon as my family left that evening, I rode my bike to the nearest convenience store. That's when I learned that convenience cost. The laxative was almost three times as much as it would have been at a Dollar General or Walmart, but those places were too far away for me to bike to, so I had no choice but to get it from there. It's a good thing I had taken a ten-dollar bill out of Mom's purse before they left. There were only two laxatives to choose from, so I bought a powdered laxative that claimed to be tasteless.

I hurried back home to mix up the concoction. I dumped a few scoops of Tang into the plastic pitcher and then added more than half of the bottle of laxative. After I added the water and a half cup of sugar, I mixed it all up with a big spoon. I tasted just a little bit to see if tasted funny, and it did. I decided to add more sugar and Tang and some dried-up lemons that fruit flies had been flying around. I gave it a few more good stirs and tried it again. It didn't taste bad. I thought I might have a new recipe. The drink looked very appetizing. The floating fruit made me want to drink a glass, but I knew better.

The next day, I slept late because I had stayed up most of the night having phone sex with the new boy in my class. I woke up to the smell of chicken and something else that smelled like heaven. My stomach was growling, and boy was my throat dry. I must have been snoring. I looked at the clock—it was well after one in the afternoon. I washed my face and went downstairs to see a table set with jerk barbecued chicken, corn bread, rice, black beans, and macaroni.

I was just in time for a fulfilling meal. Dad set the table while Mom fixed everyone's plate - they were still married back then. I offered to fill all of the glasses with ice and set them by the place settings. I poured everyone some of the Tang and had a seat. Like always, Mom and Dad went on and on about Melody this and Melody that. My older sister Raven gave my punch two thumbs up as she fixed herself and Mom another glass. I beamed with gratitude. I'd finally gotten a compliment, and I couldn't believe it. I smiled and pretended to drink some of the evil concoction from my glass.

In the middle of the night, I woke up to the sound of footsteps outside my bedroom door. I heard Melody complaining to Dad that her stomach was hurting. Dad said that Mom had been in and out of their bathroom all night, and that's where she was now. I got up and pretended that my stomach was hurting too. As soon as Raven opened the bathroom door in the hallway, a foul odor came out. I rushed in before Melody could get there. I turned the fan on in the bathroom and held my nose while I sat on the side of the bathtub. I counted to five hundred before I flushed the toilet, washed my hands, and came out.

Melody was sitting on the floor holding her stomach when I opened the door. She crawled into the bathroom and shut the door behind her. Just then, Mom walked up with a big cup of Tang and asked if my stomach was hurting too. "Yes," I replied. She then proceeded to talk to Melody through the door and told her she'd brought her something to drink so she wouldn't get dehydrated. I just walked back to my room with a smirk on my face. I fell asleep pretty quickly, but I kept being woken up by footsteps and flushing toilets.

Now, after sitting and dwelling on my shadow of a life for a few minutes, I burst out laughing and decided I better get my behind ready for school before Mom came back upstairs. I took a two-minute shower and dashed into my walk-in closet to play I Spy. *Okay*, I thought, *I spy a large BCBG bag on the top shelf.* I had forgotten about the three outfits that Stanley had gotten me last week. Stanley was an older guy who liked to spend time with me when his wife worked second shift at the hospital. That biddy was the head nurse. If she found out about all the things that Stanley and I did and all of her money that he spent on me, she probably would have a heart attack. Then all of those nurses that she bossed around on a regular basis would be nursing her back to her health.

Out of the three outfits, I chose to wear a fitted knit coral sweater and cream-colored stretch boot-cut jeans. I added my brown Steve Madden boots that Jerry bought me and my six gold bangles to complete my outfit. I dashed across the hallway to the bathroom to brush my teeth and put my hair in a quick ponytail. I then sprayed myself twice with my Victoria's Secret body spray. I smelled good and looked good too. *Hot damn!* I thought. *I am so sexy.*

When I got downstairs, I saw my mirror image sitting on our cranberry leather sectional, going over some notes. She probably was going to get an A-plus on whatever it was she was studying for. Melody was always studying, and she never received anything less than an A. I would be happy if I got a C-minus on my report card, but D's seemed to be very fond of me.

When I entered the den, I could tell that Boogie had just walked through the door because his footprints were still embedded in our soft carpet. Boogie was our neighbor; he lived four houses down from us. His real name was Roscoe, but everyone called him Boogie because he knew how to dance. He was very handsome and popular. He had brown skin and brown eyes to match. Boogie still had his braces, which he'd had on since the tenth grade because he had a habit of eating ice and eating sticky candy. The girls at our school were crazy over Boogie; I could only imagine how it was going to be when he got his braces taken off the next month.

2

School Daze

We made it to school on time, but I saw Dana in the parking lot and had to stop and see what she had for me. Dana was my go-to girl. She had stuff stored in her locker or in the trunk of her white 2008 BMW 325xi—brand-spanking-new right off the lot. Dana's dad was a plastic surgeon, and he bought her and her mom whatever they wanted. I still hadn't figured out why Dana stole; maybe it was some kind of fetish. She stole only things that could go under clothes, like bras, panties, bathing suits, stockings, and socks. As long as she kept stealing, I was always going to have the sexiest undies.

Dana looked rich, smelled rich, and dressed rich. She wore nothing but Ralph Lauren and had beach-blonde hair and the greenest eyes I'd ever seen. If I worked at a store, she would be the last person I would be worried about stealing something. She just looked so innocent.

We had been friends since ninth grade, when we had a few classes together. From then on, we were pretty tight. I'd stayed over at Dana's house a couple of times. She lived in a huge mansion, like something you would see on *MTV Cribs*. Her bedroom was in the basement, but it looked like an apartment. It had a kitchen, a master bedroom, a bathroom, and a projection screen with seating for ten. It even had a laundry room. She only had to go into the main house to exit the premises.

This time I got only a few pairs of Victoria's Secret underwear from Dana. I told her I would get more of everything when I got some more money from Stanley, or in other words when his wife got paid. As soon as I stepped through the unguarded metal detectors, the bell sounded. The last thing I'd wanted to do was be late.

As I entered the class, all eyes were on me and not because I was so gorgeous, but because I was late again. If I haven't mentioned it, my mother is African American, and my father is 100 percent Puerto Rican. People say I look like a mix between Christina Milian and Meagan Good. I couldn't be a body double for either of those beautiful ladies, but I am definitely easy on the eyes.

When my mom and dad made me, they made a melting pot of beautiful. I am a sassy, fast-dancing, no-tan-needed, no-weaves-or-perms type of girl—and not a pad-a-panty type either. I am curvy, and I have my fair share of hips and thighs since both run in my family. I have a flat stomach and more than a few handfuls of ass. Hell, if I stripped, I could make enough money to buy me one of those BMWs like Dana had.

When I entered the classroom, Mr. Mal had a smirk on his face and asked to see me after class. I knew exactly what that was about. After the bell sounded to end class, I met with Mr. Mal. Only it wasn't the top half of Mr. Mal I was meeting with; it was the bottom half. I was positioned under his desk. That way, if anybody walked into the classroom, I wouldn't be seen. He came in less than a minute, and this was the only thing that I was thankful for about my encounters with Mr. Mal.

At the water fountain I gagged at the thought of what I'd just done. I had to do it, though. If I had anymore unexcused tardies or absences,

I was going to fail Mr. Mal's class, and I needed it to graduate. Mr. Mal was very unattractive. He was a plaid-wearing, overweight, hairy pervert. He smelled like coffee and cheap cologne. *If I'm late again*, I thought, *I'm going to kill myself. I'm not going through that shit again.*

My face was flushed, and I still felt like I had to puke. While digging in my locker for my history book, I saw my mirror image talking to her non-dressing best friend Raquel. That girl didn't have the first clue about fashion. I rolled my eyes at the both of them and headed to my next class.

The rest of the day zoomed by, and I was in my psychology class before I knew it. While the teacher passed out our test from last week, I looked in my bag for my MAC lip gloss. I found it and noticed that my cell phone had three missed calls. I couldn't wait to see who it was, so I asked to be excused to go to the restroom.

When I got to the restroom, I went into the first stall. I always went into the first stall because for some reason I thought many people didn't use it. Two of the missed calls were from Stanley, and one was from my mom. Stanley wanted to spend time with me later that night because his wife was working an extra shift. Mom's message informed me that she was going out of town on business and would be gone when we got home.

I began plotting how I was going to spend my evening with my sugar daddy. I knew I was going to wear one of the panty sets that I had gotten from Dana. That covered Friday night, but I didn't know what I was going to do on Saturday. I thought about calling Jerry, but his wife had been coming home early from work a lot lately, and I wasn't trying to get caught. What really had my wheels turning the most was what Mom had planned. I knew there was more to it than just business. There had to be pleasure involved.

Usually, when Mom went on these business trips, she went with her boss Desmond. He was the owner and CEO of an advertising company

called Do Tell. He was remarkably delicious-looking, stood about 6'2",
had chocolate skin, and was built like a Greek god. Did I mention that he
was married? Now, I honestly didn't know whether they were messing
around. I didn't know whether Mom would cheat with a married man
since Dad had cheated on her, and that's why they were divorced now.
All I knew was that they traveled overnight together, and Mom always
came back nicer than ever.

On my way back to class, I saw Raquel in the hall. She asked if I was
coming with Melody to the Sugar Shack on Saturday night. I replied,
"Hell yeah! Melody's going to the Sugar Shack?" Before I could say
anything else, Raquel sprinted back to her locker. That sounded like a
plan to me. Now I had something to do on Saturday.

I'd always wanted to go to that club. Thanks to Raquel, we could
finally get in because her uncle was the new head of security. I walked
back to psychology class happy, thinking about what I might wear to
the Sugar Shack. As soon as I sat down at my desk, I saw my test. I was
happy to see that it hadn't been murdered by the infamous red pen. I had
missed only four questions and had gotten a B. That was an improve-
ment because on my last test I'd made a D.

School was over, and I was glad. I was ready to spend some time with
Stanley. I realized that I hadn't told Melody that Mom was going out
of town for the weekend yet. I knew Melody didn't know about Mom's
out-of-town trip because she didn't have a cell phone. She said she didn't
want one because they were a distraction, and if anybody needed to reach
her, they could call for her on the house phone. I figured that Melody
would probably end up blowing Raquel off and stay home so that she
could study. Not me, though, because while Sasha Russo was gone, I was
going to enjoy every single minute of it.

I knew Melody would be in the parking lot with Boogie and Raquel
since she didn't have any practice today. I walked through the commons

area, out the doors that had the graduating class of 2008's signatures all over it, down a long cement walkway, and finally to the parking lot. There she was, my mirror image, just as pretty as me without the stylish clothes, lip gloss, bangles, and makeup.

Melody was indeed with her sidekicks Boogie and Raquel. While Raquel and Boogie recapped the events that had led up to the food fight that had taken place during lunch, I talked to Melody about Mom. When we loaded up the car, I let Raquel sit in the front. I figured I better be nice to her since she was getting us into the hottest club in the city for free.

As soon as we got home, Melody laid the keys on the granite counter and started peeling off her clothes. I could tell she was going into her sandwich, shower, and study mode. She did the same thing just about every day. She kept her head in the books, every chance she could. Since Melody had practice at least two times a week for cheerleading and volleyball, she didn't want to lag behind in her studies. Melody was the captain of both teams, and if that wasn't enough, she babysat children and walked pets for the people in our close-knit neighborhood.

I wondered how she did it and how she could stay so focused. I felt the need to ask her questions. Secretly, I yearned to get to know her and hoped that we could stop living like strangers. I wanted to understand her, and I wanted her to understand me. I wanted to share my secrets with her, but I didn't want her to look down on me and tell Mom about my scandalous behavior.

I decided to let Melody do her thing, and I went upstairs to shower to get fresh for Stanley. I decided to wear a hot-pink and black panty set. I rubbed cherry-blossom body butter all over myself and sprayed perfume near the places he liked to kiss. As I stood in front of my three-way mirror, I wondered how Melody could have a body like this and not flaunt it. I was satisfied with the way I looked, so I grabbed some jogging pants and a running jacket to slip on. On the outside I looked like I was going jogging, but underneath I was dressed for a long cuddle session. Before I left, I grabbed the keys off the counter and told Melody I was going to hang out with Dana.

When I reached Stanley's house, it was almost dark. The sun was setting, and the sky was so pretty. I didn't know why, but I couldn't stop thinking about Stanley's wife. Was she giving someone medicine? Taking semen samples from a rape victim? Giving her nurses a hard time? Or simply just wondering what her husband was doing? I knew that this was wrong, but I just couldn't turn around now. I had driven all of this way. Besides, my kitty couldn't wait to see Stanley.

When I got inside, the warm earth tones on the walls melted away my thoughts of Stanley's wife. Stanley kissed me as soon as he closed the entry door. He didn't waste any time before he had me butt naked. I could tell that his wife hadn't given him any in the past two weeks because he was like an animal. He was slapping my ass, pulling my hair, and licking me from top to bottom. When it was over, it was after twelve o'clock in the morning.

As I was about to leave, Stanley pulled a box wrapped with gold paper out of his robe pocket. My eyes got big. I hadn't been expecting anything. I took the box and opened it slowly to find two gold bangles. I smiled and thought, *This makes eight now.* I hadn't gotten all of the bangles from Stanley, just these two. Every guy I messed around with bought me them because they knew I adored the shiny bracelets.

When I got home, Melody was asleep on the couch in front of our big-screen TV. There were several college applications over her instead of a blanket. I shook my head and turned the TV off. When I got in my bed that night, I thought about what I was going to do after I graduated in a few months. I hadn't applied to any schools, and I didn't have any special talents or any favorite subjects. I made my mind up that night that I wasn't going to college. I didn't think it would be hard to find a job with just a diploma. The way things were looking, I might not even need a job because my sugar daddies kept my cash flow coming.

3

Sugar Shack Saturday

The next morning, I was so sore. I would have to tell Stanley not to be so rough next time, if there was a next time. I was hoping he would put money in my bank account today like he'd said he would. Tonight was the night we were going to the Sugar Shack. I had to get my nails done and find a cute outfit. At first I wasn't going to ask my mirror image if she wanted to go with me, but something told me to ask. When she said yes, I couldn't believe it. *Maybe we can bond today*, I thought.

It was a good thing I checked the mail before we left because Dad had sent us some money. Now I didn't have to rely on Stanley to sponsor this trip to the mall. Our first stop was the day spa, where we each got a pedicure and got our brows waxed. It was Melody's first time, and when the lady snatched the wax strip off of Melody's brow, a tear ran down her cheek. I patted her on the back and told her the pain was going to be worth it in the end. As my acrylic nails were painted fire-engine red, Melody sat beside me and watched.

I was surprised that Melody was talking so much. She talked mostly about school work and graduation. Which was totally fine with me, I was happy she was finally opening up. Maybe it was the aromatherapy candles and sounds of nature music that were making her so talkative. Who knows? Next, we went to a place called Screaming Mina's. There were so many freaky clothes that I wanted to drain my bank account and go on a shopping spree. I got a few items while Melody hung out close to the exit. I could tell she was uncomfortable and ready to go.

Our next stop was the mall. We went to Bebe, Guess, Macy's, and Aldo's. I tried on everything and ended up purchasing a black catsuit with some red high heels. I never did see what Melody had bought. I guess I was trying on too much stuff. We ended up talking more over junk food from the food court. I was really enjoying my sister. I was glad she'd finally pulled herself away from the books to hang with me.

By eight thirty we were on our way home and excited more than ever about the Sugar Shack. I asked Melody to stop by the ATM so that I could check the balance on my account. When we got to the bank, I got out and quickly punched in my code. Stanley had come through: I had an extra three hundred bucks. I hopped back in the car with a huge smile. I thought about how I was going to spend this money while my sister drove the speed limit and stopped at every yellow light on the way home.

Back at the house, we turned the music on and danced around to kill time. Melody called Boogie to remind him that we would be leaving around ten thirty. Believe it or not, I was dressed and downstairs waiting on Melody when the time came. I was looking in the mirror, thinking how fierce I looked, when there was a knock on the door. I knew it was Boogie, so I just opened it.

To my surprise it wasn't Boogie. It was some other handsome guy, someone I had never seen before. He introduced himself as Boogie's cousin; his name was J.R. I let him in and told him to have a seat. Boogie came in just as I was about to shut the door. He told me that his cousin just moved here and that he wanted to show him a good time tonight. I wanted to get to know J.R. better and I wanted to show him a good time too. From what I saw, I wanted to jump his bones already.

J.R.'s skin was the color of new copper, and he had a low fade and the straightest teeth I had ever seen. When he walked past me, I noticed that he had a sense of fashion. He was wearing the latest Sean John casual apparel. I also noticed the print of his penis through the thin material of his pants. All I could think was *yummy*. But although I was checking J.R. out like I was about to drive him off a car lot, he paid me no attention whatsoever. What man wouldn't notice me, standing here in this damn catsuit and these high-ass heels on? I thought, *He has to be gay.*

As soon as I started pouting, Melody made her way downstairs. Even I was speechless. She looked amazing. She wore a hot-pink low-cut top and a black miniskirt. Her ass was bigger than mine, but I'd never known it. I couldn't believe my eyes, and it seemed J.R. couldn't either because his eyes were off of our big-screen TV and on Melody. I could tell he was interested in her when he kissed her hand and introduced himself.

When we got to the Sugar Shack, we parked and immediately saw Raquel. I have to admit, this was the only time I had ever been happy to see her. Raquel looked cute, but of course, she had nothing on me. As soon as we stepped in the Shack, girls were hating. I could see the looks on their faces. My catsuit was killing them softly. All of the attention made me horny.

Before we got to our booth, some skank had snatched up Boogie, and even Raquel was popping her no-ass on some cutie with braids. I looked over to tell Melody to check out her friend shaking what her momma gave her. That's when I noticed Melody and J.R. were cuddled up in the damn corner. I felt like I should have stayed home. I decided to walk around a little to see if I could find the ladies' room. Maybe I could get some conversation out of the attendant at least.

Just as I was about to walk into the ladies' room, someone grabbed my hand and said, "Where have you been? I have been looking all over for you."

I turned around to see a fine chocolate drop. I'd never seen him before, and I didn't know who he was or where he had come from. I replied, "I'm going to the ladies' room. Would you like to come with me?"

A smile so bright came up on the stranger's face; he knew I was joking and apparently was happy to see that I had a sense of humor. He handed me a ticket and told me to come to the VIP room when I was done in the ladies' room. I shook my head okay and went to the ladies' room to check my lip gloss and push my boobs up. After primping in the mirror for three minutes or so, I headed right to the VIP room.

When the guard opened the door, I was amazed at what I saw. There was a bar, a dance floor, and black walls plastered with mirrors. When I saw the guy who had given me the VIP pass, he motioned for me to come over. As I sat beside him on the cold leather, he asked me what my name was, and I told him. He told me that his name was Mont and that he was twenty-one. From there the conversation got deeper, and I soon felt like I had known him for years. He made me laugh, I felt comfortable, and I was so happy that he had approached me.

It was getting late. As much as I hated to, I had to cut the conversation short, so I could go back to meet up with Melody, J.R., and Boogie. Mont didn't want me to go, and he agreed to take me home. I told him that I needed to go tell my sister not to wait for me. On the way back to the booth, I smiled and thought that not that long ago, I had been in a smoke-filled room in a booth with people who probably hadn't even noticed I was gone. When I reached the booth, Melody and J.R. were still in the corner, all hugged up. I told them not to wait up and that a friend was going to bring me home soon. They shook their heads, and I was off to the VIP room once again.

Mont and I sat and talked for a few more hours. I was really digging him. We had a lot in common. On top of all that, Mont owned a customized Mercedes with his name stitched in the seats. He was super cute, he knew how to dress, and he looked like he could eat the hell out of some kitty. I couldn't wait to see what he was packing.

On the way to my house, we decided to grab some breakfast. We talked even more, and I was surprised that Mont hadn't said anything about sex. Maybe he was a different type of guy. At my front door he kissed me on the cheek, and I felt like I was going to melt. I gave him a hug and told him to call me and let me know when he got home.

When I walked in the house, there was complete silence. I couldn't believe that Melody wasn't on the couch asleep with the TV blasting. I thought, *She must've really been tired.* In the shower all I could think about was Mont. Afterward, I put on my pajamas and decided to go check on my mirror image. When I looked in Melody's room, I saw size eleven feet hanging off the bed. Clothes were everywhere, and the smell of sex was in the air. Oh my goodness. Melody slept with J.R.! I couldn't believe my goody-two-shoes sister had done something Mom wouldn't approve of. I'd gotten enough of an eyeful for one night. I shook my head in disbelief as I walked to my bedroom.

I was startled out of my slumber when I felt something shaking my bed. When I turned to see what was going on, Melody was stuffing J.R. under my bed. They both were breathing rapidly. Melody whispered, "Mom's in the driveway. Go along with me please."

I replied, "Okay, but it's too early for this shit, girl." I looked at the clock, and it was almost eight in the morning. I'd gotten into bed only three hours ago. I turned on my TV, and Melody and I lay there pretending to watch some dumb early morning show.

When Mom opened the door and saw the both of us, her eyes widened because this was definitely out of the ordinary. Melody had never really come in my room and stayed. I couldn't recall her even ever sitting on my bed. She would only come and borrow a shirt or something and then make a speedy exit.

"What are you doing back?" I said sleepily.

She replied, "Desmond's son was in a car accident early this morning." She then walked over and sat down in between us. She hugged both of us and kissed Melody first and then me. Mom's eyes were getting glossy, and I could tell she was about to cry. I suggested that she needed some rest and shooed her out of the room.

We gladly watched Mom make her exit. I followed her to her room, lit her candles, and ran her a bath. I didn't leave Mom's room until she was getting into the tub. I quickly walked down the hall back to my bedroom. J.R. was lying on the floor, and Melody was on top of him, kissing him. I could only imagine what had happened last night. I whispered, "We need to get J.R. out of the house now, because Mom is in the tub." Melody didn't listen; she just kept on kissing him.

I didn't know what to do. I had never seen Melody act this way. I knew that Mom wouldn't be in the bath long because she looked so tired. Since they couldn't keep their hands off each other, I decided to crack my bedroom door so that I could watch out for Mom. When thirty minutes had passed, I decided to go and see if Mom was asleep. I tiptoed down the carpeted hall and pushed Mom's bedroom door open with ease. Even though her candles were lit, she was out like a light.

Yet again, I walked quickly and quietly down the hallway back to my bedroom. I pulled Melody off of J.R. and said, "Stop it. He has to go now!" After the scolding we all headed downstairs. Before J.R. left, he and Melody shared the longest kiss I had ever seen in real life. Once he was gone, I let out a deep sigh of relief, and suddenly, my headache was gone from hiding a knucklehead in the house. Melody made me swear that I wouldn't tell Mom about what had happened. I told her I wouldn't swear unless she told me everything.

Instantly, Melody started pouring her guts out to me, and I couldn't believe it. She said, "He smelled so damn good. It's like he had me hypnotized. I really like him, Lyric; you know that I would never do anything like this in any of my lifetimes. I think that J.R. is my soul mate."

I replied, "Are you serious? You just met him. I thought you were smarter than that. You don't know anything about this guy. I've heard enough." I got up and headed to the patio to try to clear my mind.

When I reached the hammock, I thought that all of my worries would swing away, but boy, was I was wrong. I felt like a hypocrite because I had just met Mont last night, and I knew without a doubt that I was in love with him already. Could it be that Melody and I had found the men of our dreams in the same night? I figured I wouldn't know unless I went back and talked to her.

On my way back inside the house, I told myself not to be so stubborn and to keep an open mind. I didn't want Melody to shut down on me. This might be my chance to finally develop a relationship with my sister. I walked through the kitchen and sat down beside my mirror image. I could tell she had been sitting there with her shoulders slumped since our last conversation.

4

Meeting Stanley's Wife

I ended up falling asleep on the couch, and I woke up to the phone ringing. I jumped up, immediately thinking it was Mont. I had my sexy voice ready. Picking up the phone, I said, "Russo residence."

The voice on the other end was raspy, with an accent. "Hi, baby," the voice replied. It was my father, Rico Russo. I was happy to talk to him because I hadn't heard from him since last week. He inquired about our graduation, which was only a few months away. I gave Dad all the info about the invitations, the yearbooks, and the cost of our caps and gowns. Just as we were about to hang up, he asked me about Mom. He wanted to know if Mom had a boyfriend or any male friends. I told him that it was none of his business.

Dad let out a giggle. He begged and pleaded with me to tell him. He even offered me money. I told him to send me a hundred bucks, and I would spill the beans about Mom and her guy friend. He agreed to send it, so I just started blabbing. I made up a man to tell Dad about. I made this man fine, established, and single. All

Dad could say was "Mm-hmm." I was about to burst from holding in my laughter when I heard a beep on the line. It was for Melody, so I told Dad I would call him back after I picked up my money from Western Union.

Do you actually think that I would rat on my own momma? Hell no! I loved my Dad and everything, but he was dead wrong for messing up our wonderful life. He just had to cheat with those models. My dad was a well-known photographer for *Rolling Stone*, *Vogue*, and many other famous magazines, magazines that you or somebody you know probably has spread out like a fan on a coffee table.

Rico Russo's skin had been French-kissed by the sun. His thick wavy hair could make you seasick if you looked at him at the right angle. Dad's blue-gray eyes often made strangers ask if he had contacts in. To tell you the truth, he could have been a model himself if he weren't so in love with taking pictures of people.

Right now Dad was living in Miami with his latest model chick. He changed girlfriends every year, it seemed. He and Mom had been divorced since Melody and I were in the eighth grade. Now we lived in Virginia. I missed living in Miami and staying with Dad, but I hadn't been back since I slapped his last girlfriend. She was bossing me around and shit, and I wasn't having that. Daddy sent me packing. He told Melody she could stay, but she decided to come with me, which surprised the hell out of me.

Life was a roller coaster with Mom. She was always comparing me to Melody. When Dad and Mom were together, it was a little easier to deal with—I guess because she was getting a good stiff one every night. I could hear them through the walls, and it made my skin crawl. That's why I used to sleep with ear plugs. When Mom and Dad were around each other now, it seemed awkward to me. I knew she still loved him, but he was such a player. I guess that's where I got it from. Anyway, I hoped that when Dad came for our graduation, he wouldn't bring one of his size-zero arm trophies.

I went upstairs to check my phone and realized it was dead. I knew that Mont had been calling me; I just knew it. When I hooked my phone up to the charger, it came back to life and started vibrating like crazy. I had missed six calls, so I knew that I had to have messages. Two calls were from Stanley, one was from Dana, and the rest were from an unavailable number. I checked my messages, and all Stanley wanted was to talk and cuddle. Dana let me know that she had been to the mall again and had more undergarments for me to look through. The other person who had called hadn't left any messages.

I was wondering who the missed calls were from when the house phone rang again. I took my sweet time getting it because I thought it was my dad again. I answered the phone with a very dry "hello."

On the other end was a faint voice. "Hello, beautiful."

I replied, "Mont, is that you?"

"Yes, it's me."

"Whatever happened to you calling me last night?" I said.

He replied, "Lyric, I am in the hospital. A drunk driver ran into me last night after I dropped you off."

I didn't know what to do or say. I froze up. While he talked, I listened carefully. Mont's voice sounded like he had been stranded in the desert without water for a day or two. As much as I told him not to strain his voice, he insisted on filling me in on the details of the accident. From what I could understand, a drunk man in a silver Mitsubishi had run a stoplight and T-boned Mont and his beautiful Mercedes.

The guy in the Mitsubishi was okay, of course—he didn't even have to go to the hospital. He went straight to jail for his second DUI. Drunk drivers never seemed to get hurt while they were driving under the influence. It was the innocent drivers who got mangled in a vehicle that ended up looking like a piece of balled-up aluminum foil. Mont had to be cut out of what was left of his car and was knocked out cold from the impact of the air bag.

I was happy to hear that Mont had no broken bones or internal bleeding. He had survived the crash with a bad case of whiplash, a few burns on his face from the airbag, and a sprained wrist. After hearing what all my new sexy had gone through, I had to go and see about him. As soon as Mont gave me his room number, I ran upstairs, put on the tightest pair of Levi's I could find, and headed to the hospital.

I couldn't find a decent parking spot, so I parked in the staff parking lot. As I walked, I thought about the condition Mont was in. I was so glad that he wasn't seriously hurt. As I walked through the revolving doors at the hospital, the smell of old people, Lysol, and stale air made me feel a little queasy. I stepped in the elevator and pushed the button. I couldn't wait to see Mont, but I had to stop by the ladies' room first so that I could primp in the mirror.

For some reason the restroom smelled like cinnamon. I put my purse on the counter and started looking for my lip gloss, chewing gum, and body spray. As I began to primp, a lady came out of the third stall. Her face was oval, and she wore hardly any makeup. Her hair was in a bun, and she was dressed to impress. She had the latest Coach bag with some killer heels to match. As she went to wash her hands, she put her purse on the counter. I noticed her car keys dangling from the side pocket of the purse. She drove a Lexus. I immediately wondered what she did for a living.

The lady left, but her perfume lingered in the restroom. I didn't know what it was, but it sure smelled expensive. I quickly got myself together and turned the corner, only to bump into a lady whose badge read RN Cyndi McKnight. It was Stanley's wife. I thought I would shit bricks. I had seen her before, but from a distance. I had never realized how pretty she was. She asked me if I needed help finding a patient. I told her yes, and she took me straight to Mont.

Mont was sitting up in the bed watching TV. When he saw me and Nurse McKnight come in the room, he said, "The world's best nurse is back, and look, she brought a beautiful young lady with her."

I smiled instantly. I was happy to see him. I hugged him and kissed him on the cheek. Other than the injuries Mont had already told me about, there were a few scrapes on his arms. As he introduced me to Cyndi McKnight, she extended her arm to shake my hand—the same hand I had used to jack off her husband the other night in the shower. At this point I felt like I was about to pass out. I thought I might need a hospital bed to lie down in.

Mont told me that she had been taking real good care of him since her shift began. Nurse McKnight explained to me why Mont was still in the hospital. I just shook my head and thought that this was so crazy. I was in the room with my new boo and my sugar daddy's wife—how strange. Her money had actually brought the stylish lightweight leather jacket I was wearing.

The hours flew by, and before I knew it, visiting hours were almost over. I tried not to squeeze Mont when I hugged him, but I couldn't help it. Mont let out a moan just as the door opened. It was Nurse McKnight and the same lady I had seen in the ladies' room when I first arrived at the hospital. Nurse McKnight was coming to tell Mont good night because her shift was about to end. The other lady had a bag that read Coco's Creations. I was wondering why the lady was there until Mont said, "Mom, you didn't have to bring me anything to eat this late." So the lady with the Lexus keys was Mont's mother. He introduced us. Mrs. Coco was nice. I could tell that she had Mont spoiled.

Just as the elevator door was about to close, Nurse McKnight put her hand in to stop the door from closing. "Guess I'll ride down with you," she said. I put on the phoniest smile I could dig up out of my soul. She started a conversation, talking about how nice my boyfriend was and shit like that. I only smiled and nodded. I was so glad when the elevator ride was over. When we reached the parking lot, I thought I was going to finally get away from her, but she kept following me. I'd forgotten that I parked in the staff parking lot. I had ended up parking directly across from her.

I tried to crank my car on, but the engine wouldn't turn. It looked like I had left my lights on again. I had a bad habit of doing that. I popped the hood and was looking under it like I knew what I was doing when Nurse McKnight asked if I needed a jump. I told her that it looked that way. She said that she would give me a jump if her jumper cables were in her hatch.

I knew that the cables were in her hatch because Stanley and I had had sex in her Jeep recently. I could remember how cold the metal from the cables was on my back when I accidentally lay back on them. While I was thinking, Nurse McKnight got the jumper cables out and hooked them up. As we were waiting for the car to get a good charge, her phone rang. She answered it on the first ring and said, "Hi, Stanley." That's when I swallowed my gum. She talked to him for a minute and told him that she had to go because she was giving a young lady a jump. She then ended the call with "Love you too."

As soon as she hung up her phone, my phone started ringing. It was Stanley's ringtone, and I didn't dare answer it. I was nauseous and sweaty, and my stomach was starting to bubble. At this point I wanted nothing more than to get in my car and haul ass. When I tried to crank my car up for the third time, the engine finally turned, and it was like music to my ears, my new favorite song in fact.

While I was driving home, I thought, *Damn, what a weekend.* I'd almost had a heart attack. My sister had lost her virginity, my new boo had escaped the Grim Reaper's scythe, and my sugar daddy's wife had just rescued me from having to wait in a dark parking lot until my mom could come for me.

5

Planning and Plotting

The following week, I learned even more about Mont. It turned out
that my mother's boss Desmond was his father. Mont's mother,
Constance, was a highly sought-after event planner, and she owned
Coco's Creations, a catering company that served everything from caviar
to chicken bog. They were living it up, they had a house almost as big as
Dana's parents, and they had an Acura, a Lexus, and a Jaguar. It looked
like I had struck gold with Mont.

I was so glad that I had gone to the Sugar Shack last weekend. I
wanted to kiss Raquel for inviting us. Being that I had school all week,
I didn't really get to spend that much time with Mont over the next few
days. Since I knew about all of the assets Desmond and Constance had, I
was beyond excited to see how Mont was living. So far I hadn't returned
any of Stanley's or Jerry's calls. I decided that I was done with the both
of them and that I wanted to be serious about my new relationship with
Mont.

I finally got a chance to see Mont's place when he was released from the hospital. It was a nice two-bedroom townhouse on the east side of town. The ceilings were high, and the walls were a bright white. The floors were a dark hardwood, and the contrast was amazing. The living room area featured a super soft rug, two multicolored armchairs, and a leather recliner and a comfy couch all set up in a conversational setting. Two matching runners in the long hallway led to the rest of the house. From what I could see, it was nice and clean, and I was secretly ready to move in. I couldn't wait to see how soft his bed was, how hot the water got in his shower, and whether he had a porn stash.

He showed me the rest of the house. The kitchen had quartz countertops and some other kind of expensive tiles. The appliances were stainless steel, and not a smudge or streak was anywhere to be seen. It looked like Mont was a neat freak. Hell, I was hoping he was a freak in the bed. When we finally got into his bedroom, it took me by surprise. The walls were a dark gray color, the bedding was black faded to red, and everything was color-coordinated. I was really impressed.

Mont instructed me to take my shoes off and make myself at home. He then lay across his king-size bed and patted the spot next to him. I lay down face-to-face with him with my hand propped under my head. That's when the conversation began. I honestly thought that we were going to have sex, but we didn't. We talked about everything—our parents, our siblings, summer camp in the seventh grade, and places we wanted to visit before we left this earth.

Like it always did, the time flew by when I was with Mont. He made me happy, and I felt like I could drown myself in him. I just couldn't get enough of that man. We cuddled a bit and exchanged a few soft kisses, but that was the only action I got out of Mont. On the way home, we stopped by Steak 'n Shake, and I ordered a chocolate shake. Mont ordered a triple cheeseburger combo. We ate and drank until we reached Stone Dale Court.

He walked me to my door and kissed me on the cheek with his greasy lips. I thought it was sweet. We agreed to go to the mall the next day and then back to his place to see if we could catch a movie on one of his hundreds of channels. I was sure we would find something to watch, and if we didn't, we could just talk. That would be fine with me.

When I got in the house, it smelled so good. I knew Mom had laid it down in the kitchen. Pots and pans were on the stove. I saw a lot of lemons in the trash can, so I knew there was fresh-squeezed lemonade in the fridge. It was a good thing I'd had only a shake. I fixed a small plate and channel-surfed. Nothing was on the tube as usual.

I decided to wash the dishes so that I wouldn't have to hear Mom's mouth. Just as I was letting the dishwater drain out of the sink, Melody came into the kitchen and asked whether I had eaten. I told her, "Yep, Mom stuck her foot in it this time."

Melody said, "Girl, I cooked for J.R."

I replied, "You cooked all of that? Damn, girl."

Melody thanked me for washing the dishes and invited me to her bedroom. After I wiped down the counters, I flicked the lights off and headed to her room to chat.

The next day, I decided to wear purple. There was something about the color that I loved. All of the shades made me feel so pretty. The mall was packed. Mont wanted to go to the food court, so we did. While he ordered a smoothie, I people-watched and wondered whether there was a sale at Dillard's. At the last minute I decided to get a parmesan pretzel; it was soft and fresh.

After we were done snacking, Mont wanted to go to Foot Locker. He bought the new Jordans and a few pairs of basketball shorts. He asked if I wanted anything, and I told him that I liked the black and white Converses. He brought them for me in a ladies' size seven. I thanked him as we exited the store. We passed by all of the window shoppers and finally reached Dillard's. I was instantly drawn to the shoe department. Mont told me to go ahead and look as he headed to the cologne counter.

I was swept away, trying on all those shoes. I ended up buying a pair of Jessica Simpson boots that were on sale for a hundred bucks. When I was finally ready to check out, I noticed Mont walking over my way with three big bags. I wondered what he had bought. On the way out of the mall, we noticed people coming inside with umbrellas. It must be been raining, we realized. Mont told me to wait at the entrance so that I wouldn't have to run to the car in the rain. I did as I was told. When I saw Mrs. Coco's Lexus pull up by the entrance, I walked out under the breezeway and got in.

Once I was inside, Mont smiled and said, "I have something special planned for you today."

I replied, "Oh really?" and kissed him softly on the lips.

It didn't take long to get to Mont's place. After turning off the engine, he retrieved the three big bags out of the backseat. He then opened my car door, and we both ran to the entry door to get out of the rain.

It was cold in the condo. We were both wet from the rain. Mont walked with me into his bathroom and flipped a switch, but the light didn't come on. I blurted out, "Did you pay your light bill?"

He laughed and replied, "Of course. I always pay my bills on time. That switch was for the heated floors."

Heated floors, I thought. *My goodness.*

After placing one of the big bags on the bathroom counter, he told me to take a shower or a bath, whichever I preferred. I started to peel off my wet jeans before Mont left the bathroom. I thought he was going to stay, but he didn't. I sighed and looked in the mirror at my nipples peeking through my thin wet shirt. I then stripped and started the shower as I wondered what he had up his sleeve.

The water was hot and steamy. There were six different spray settings in the luxurious shower. I made sure every inch of my body was clean and fresh. I grabbed a towel and stepped out on the warm tile, dried off, and grabbed the big bag on the counter. The first thing I saw was a familiar looking box. I opened it to see a gold bangle. After smiling at myself in the mirror, I slipped it onto my arm with the others, and continued to dig in the bag. I liked what I saw, when I pulled out a lavender robe with a slip nightgown that matched. It was a sexy little get up and I loved that they were both trimmed in dark purple lace. The bag also contained some lotion and some cute purple, furry high-heeled slippers. I popped the tags off of everything and lathered the sweet smelling lotion on my body.

When I opened the bathroom door, I smelled a wonderful aroma. I walked in the kitchen to find Mont pouring red wine into two wine glasses. I really wasn't expecting anything like this. We had baked chicken, loaded mashed potatoes, and steamed squash. Someone must have delivered the food from his mom's catering company while I was in the shower. During our meal, Mont complemented me on how I looked and smelled. The wine had me buzzed, and I was so horny.

After dinner Mont ushered me into the living room. He turned on a movie and sat down beside me. As soon as he sat down, I climbed on top of him and gave him a big hug. He hugged me back and smiled. I kissed his neck and ears. He started caressing my back and behind. I could tell he was hard—I could feel it through his jeans. I started grinding on him. When I took off my robe, I slid my arms out of the straps of the nightgown, and my breasts were in his face. He kissed and rubbed them. Then he flipped me over and started sucking on my neck.

Unfortunately, that was all that happened because Mont stopped and said that it was too early in the relationship to go this far. He then apologized for leading me on. I tried to tell him that it was okay, but he had already jumped up and sat in the recliner. I really didn't know how to feel about this. I finally talked Mont into coming back to the couch with me after I had put the robe back on. He held me while we watched a movie. With the sun now shining through the blinds, all I could do was think about Stanley. My heart was here with Mont, but my kitty wanted to be in that brownstone in the neighboring city.

6

Graduation-Bound

A fter my first bangle from Mont, the time flew by. The weather was warm, and I was letting it all hang out. My life was going well, and even my grades were a little better. Mont and I were officially a couple, and Melody and I had a close relationship now. I felt really horrible for doing so many mean things to her while we were growing up. I had bleached her favorite bedding; taken money out of her piggy bank; stuck her toothbrush in the toilet; put weed in her backpack at school, hoping the drug dog would sniff it out; put itching powder in her underwear drawer; and even shredded her acceptance letters from a few colleges that she was interested in attending.

Those are just a few of the mean things I did to my mirror image. I was so jealous that I didn't care how I hurt her. I wished now that I could take it all back. I couldn't believe that I had stooped so low, and I was truly ashamed of myself. I hoped she would never find out about any of the things I'd done. If she did, I was sure that she would never talk to me again. I decided to pray and ask the good Lord for forgiveness. I also thanked him for the new relationship that Melody and I had. The praying made me feel better instantly. I now realized how much I adored my mirror image.

Cap and gown time was approaching and Mont still wasn't giving anything up. That forced me to go to Stanley. He was still into me and wondered why I had neglected him. I told him I was stressed out from school. He accepted the lame excuse and couldn't wait to caress me all over. We hooked up a few times. The sex was good, but I would have much rather had Mont in between my legs than a forty-plus-year-old man with graying edges.

The yearbooks were ordered, and invitations were mailed out. A lot of our family was coming to see us graduate. I was kind of worried because Daddy was bringing his girlfriend. I hoped this wouldn't bother Mom too much. I crossed my fingers that everything would work out.

Mom and Melody were ecstatic because she had received six full scholarship offers. All Melody had to do was make up her mind up about which school she wanted to go to, and she would be on her way to receiving a bachelor's degree. I couldn't honestly say that I was happy for my sister. I had to admit there was just a tiny bit of jealousy left in me toward her.

I knew that Melody had worked hard and studied hard for her 4.6 grade point average. I couldn't help but think that I had made a big mess out of my high school years—C's and D's, cutting school, tardiness, and discipline referrals. If I would have applied myself, I could have been going off to college somewhere too. I knew Mom was going to be proud of me just for graduating, but I realized now that I'd let myself down by not giving my all.

The last month of school went by so slow. The classes were long, boring, and pointless. I was glad when they called everyone out of class who had ordered a yearbook. I wanted to roam the halls for autographs from the football and basketball players. Boogie was the first to crack my book open and sign it. While I was signing his, he said, "That page with you and Melody is off the hook."

"What are you talking about?" I asked.

He replied, "Flip near the back of the book, and you'll see it."

Well, I'll be damned, I thought. There it was—a whole page of just me and Melody. Snaggletoothed, on bikes, in bathtubs, and on our first day of school. There was even a neat twin poem in the center of the page. I was so surprised to see this. We looked so cute. I knew this had to have cost a lot of money, and I wondered why Melody hadn't told me about it.

As soon as I closed Boogie's book, Melody sat down beside me. She said, "Did you see it?"

I replied, "Yes, and I love it." I gave her a big hug. I knew I was going miss her when she left for college. Soon after Melody joined Boogie and me, there was an announcement calling Melody to the main office. She looked surprised. I walked with her up to the office. Mrs. Johnson told Melody that her guidance counselor wanted to talk to her.

I stayed put in an old club chair because I knew that I was supposed to be back in class by now. When Melody returned, there were tears running down her face. "Melody what's wrong?" I asked.

She replied, "I just found out that I am the valedictorian."

I smiled as she wiped her tears away with her hands. Everything she had worked so hard for was worth the feeling she had now. I knew Mom was going to flip out.

I separated myself from my sister and took the long way back to class. Just after I passed Dana's locker, they made an announcement for Claire Bullard to come to the main office. I figured that lucky duck was the salutatorian. When I got back to class, the students weren't doing anything. There was a movie on, but most people were signing yearbooks. When I sat down, Dana complimented me on my bathtub photo. I looked in her green eyes and replied, "Thank you. That was Melody's idea."

That night Mom took us out to dinner. We talked and caught up with her, and I felt free with my mom and sister; I had no worries. We talked about the sleeping arrangements and who was staying where for graduation. We had everything planned out. I was ready to see my sister Raven and my three-year-old twin nieces. They were all going to be sleeping with Mom because Raven's husband couldn't come. Mom's three sisters were staying in Raven's old bedroom. Mom had a futon and some old wooden bunk beds set up in there.

Dad was coming, but he was staying at a hotel not too far from our house with his girlfriend. He was also bringing Papa, Nana, Uncle Luis, and Aunt Maria. I couldn't wait to see them. I knew we were going to rack up presents and cash. It crossed my mind that Melody was going to get more attention than I was because of the scholarships and the valedictorian situation. I just put that in the back of my mind and tried to not let the jealousy leak out of me.

I saw Mont only a little this week because he was busy helping his mom at her catering company. He said that they had a lot of graduation parties lined up. I could believe it because as hot as it was, nobody was trying to cook. I was glad he was helping his mom, but I needed some help in the sex department. I was kind of tired of being with Stanley. Deep down, I felt sorry for his wife. She worked so hard, and all Stanley did was run around on her. I had to stop this because I didn't want to lose Mont over this Stanley situation. I had to tell Mont soon that I needed sex. I just didn't know how to tell him.

7

Getting Closer

I managed to get a job three weeks before graduation. I would be a waitress at a place called Island Getaway, which served the best wings in town. The attire there was kind of like Hooters, but the shorts weren't quite as short. I knew I was going to get the job because the manager couldn't keep his eyes off of my boobs during the interview. I knew exactly what I was doing when I wore a low-cut blouse and one of the push-up bras I had gotten from Dana.

It only took me a few days to learn all of the specials and the menu. After that, I was a natural. I kept a huge smile on my face, and I kept wearing those push-up bras. If I had to wait on a couple or a group of ladies, I always complimented the ladies on their purses, jewelry, or outfits; that way, they wouldn't feel intimidated by the combination of good looks and booty I had. If I waited on a group of guys, I made my lips extra pouty and added extra lip gloss. That kept the tips coming in.

I was averaging about one hundred bucks a night in tips. I never thought I could make so much money at a dead-end job like this. It looked like I wouldn't need any money from Stanley or Jerry again, if the customers continued to tip this well. While making money was on my mind, I often thought about how my life would be once Melody left for college.

I finally made my mind up about applying to the community college. I know I said that I wasn't going to college, but that was before I found out that Melody had these scholarship offers. When I first saw Mom and Melody jumping up and down, I was happy. Now I felt hella jealous. I honestly didn't know what had gotten into me again.

I thought I was okay. I hated the fact that I had evil thoughts about doing something bad to Melody. I needed to go to a therapist or something. I felt like I couldn't control myself, and what was going on inside of me was really unhealthy. I was always fighting with what was right and wrong on the inside. I definitely needed to pray about it because meditating hadn't been working.

I loved my sister, and I knew I was going to miss her so much. Maybe what it all boiled down to was that I was going to be lonely. She was leaving me, her mirror image. This was going to be real hard, but I decided to talk to Melody and tell her how I felt. After my shift I asked Melody to come and talk to me in my closet. She looked at me like I was crazy, but she followed me.

In the closet I let it all out. We talked about J.R., Mont, Momma, Dad, school, and anything and everything else. My sister opened up to me and told me that she had almost six thousand dollars in the bank. She said that she had been saving since she was ten, and she broke it all down, explaining how the money had added up. Melody had been saving from tooth fairy visits, elementary and middle school graduations, the odd jobs she did around the neighborhood, allowances, birthday presents, and child support from Dad.

I felt numb. The green-eyed monster was about to rear its ugly head again. I just couldn't shake this thing. I hardly had a thousand bucks in my savings account. I felt so stupid. I had been spending my money on nails, designer shades, and clothes all throughout high school. All Melody did was borrow my clothes and shop at the Salvation Army. Thinking about how much cash I had wasted made my stomach hurt. If I had saved like she had, I would have been sitting pretty right about now.

When I first started high school, I had a dozen upper-class male friends who used to give me money all of the time—not for sex, but just because. However, I did sleep with quite a few of them. I had so much jewelry, clothes, shoes, and makeup that it was ridiculous. Half of the girls at school hated my guts, and the other half wanted to be me. At school people would say Melody and I were nothing alike. They said that if we weren't twins, people wouldn't even have known that we were sisters.

Melody was always on time, she made all A's, and she was head of the publication staff, the homecoming queen, and damn near everything else. I, on the other hand, was always late, didn't participate in any school activities, and was happy if I made all C's. I hardly ever made A's unless one of my teachers and I had something worked out. One guy used to jack off while I stuck my thumb in and out of his butt. I didn't think that was too bad for an A. Besides, Mom was always happy when I brought home an A in anything.

Speaking of Mom, she had just gotten back from another business trip. She was all smiles and even had a tan. I wondered where Mom and Desmond really went. Melody and I speculated about what the real deal was between them. I honestly hoped that there wasn't anything going on. Since I was dating Desmond's son, this was going to be a sticky situation if they were involved. I didn't know where things were going with Mont, but I was curious to find out.

Anyway, Mont and I were still chopping it up, and things were getting pretty serious. I made sure I split my time on my days off between Mont and Melody equally. It felt great hanging out with my sister. I sure wished that we could have bonded earlier.

8

Hats Off

Finally, the last day of school arrived. I was so happy to get up that morning. Mom was surprised when she didn't have to fuss at me about getting up and being late. Today was the senior cookout, and I was going to be outside rambling all day—eating hot dogs and hamburgers and flirting with all the fine ballplayers one last time. All week Melody had been working on her speech and had been uninvolved with everything and anyone else, including J.R. He was used to a lot of Melody's attention, but lately he had been hanging out with Raquel. Melody didn't care because she had to get her graduation speech together.

Over the next couple days, envelopes in all colors, shapes, and sizes arrived in our mailbox—cards from our relatives who couldn't make it to our graduation for various reasons. They were proud of us and showed their enthusiasm by sending us checks, cash, and gift cards. I was loaded with dough, and none of it was from Stanley or Jerry.

The day before graduation came, and so did our relatives. The house was full, and we were enjoying everybody. There were conversations going on in Spanglish and southern slang. Dad had brought a beautiful almond-eyed girl with a long black expensive weave. She also had the latest Dooney and Bourke bag that cost at least four hundred bucks. I knew that Daddy had bought the weave and the bag. I hated that Dad couldn't spot gold diggers.

❧

It was hot, and I had just sat down beside my sister on the football field. We were wearing our white caps and gowns. The time had come for Melody to give her valedictorian speech, and I think I was more nervous than she was. When she walked to the podium, she adjusted the microphone and cleared her throat. She delivered a speech that had our family and friends yelling, "That's right!" and "You go, girl!" from the audience. I thought some of the people were going to get kicked out because of the "clap only and no yelling" rule that the administrators had warned us all about at the beginning of the ceremony.

I didn't think there was a dry eye in the crowd after Melody delivered the speech. She talked about the importance of letting your light shine, she took it all the way back to elementary school, she even mentioned bullying and putting your best foot forward. The graduating class of four hundred–plus was floored by the speech. I knew they were proud that Melody was representing us as the graduating class of 2008. It was an honor to be her sister, and I wasn't the least bit upset that the silent tears I cried during her speech had ruined my makeup.

Before I knew it, the speech that Melody had taken so long to prepare was over, and everyone was on their feet and clapping. She was back at her seat in a flash, only to see tears still streaming down my face. Melody reached over, gave me a big hug, and handed me a Kleenex that she had tucked in her bra. I cleaned up as well as I could with one hand while Melody tightly squeezed the other.

When it was time for our row to stand up and get our diplomas, my legs were like Jell-O. When my name was called, it seemed like I was walking in slow motion, and everything was quiet. As I walked across the stage, I strutted my stuff the best I could—everybody knew I had a killer shape under that big white gown. I went borderline cuckoo inside my head when the principal handed me the square jacket cover that held my precious diploma. I kissed the diploma and held it up high.

Back in my seat, my mind was running wild. I thought about our graduation party back at the house. I couldn't stop thinking about all of the fruit trays, finger sandwiches, punch, and of course, presents. I snapped out of it as the principal was making his last speech. After he instructed the class of 2008 to move our tassels to the other side of our graduation caps, everyone went wild. We all hugged, cheered, screamed, and jumped up and down.

I kicked my shoes off as soon as we got home. I couldn't wait to get out of those heels. I took a quick shower and made a mad dash back to my room with one of Dana's Ralph Lauren towels wrapped around me. When I stepped into my closet, I heard quiet crying. I looked over to my left and saw Melody sitting on one of my old gym bags. I immediately knelt down and said, "What's wrong?"

It took her a few minutes to get herself together and reply. "I'm pregnant."

I didn't know what to say at first. I couldn't believe this.

Melody then said, "I didn't have a period last month. I thought it was stress from school, but when I took a pregnancy test, it came back positive."

"What are you going to do?" I asked.

"Lyric, I have to abort. I can't go to college pregnant, and I'm not ready for a child."

I tried my best to console Melody. I told her that people were waiting on us to come downstairs so that they could shower us with gifts. I suggested that we look for places to abort later on tonight after everything settled down. I then went into the bathroom and returned to my closet with a warm washcloth. I wiped Melody's face and gave her a big hug. After I got dressed, Melody and I held hands and walked downstairs together.

The food was good, but the gift table had my attention. Balloons were everywhere, and so were my three-year-old twin nieces Paris and London. I didn't know what Raven was going to do with those girls. Aunt Mona grabbed the twins, sat them down in front of the television, and turned on some kiddie channel, and the twins were in hog heaven. I was happy—we could finally open our presents without the little boogers getting in the way.

I sat beside Mont and listened to my mom tell a funny story about Melody and me when we were younger. Everyone was laughing, and I could tell that Mont was enjoying this. I sat beside him and listened with a smile on my face until it was finally time to open the presents. I unwrapped perfume, gift cards, jewelry, and cold hard cash—those gifts were from aunts, uncles, Granny, and Papa.

Mom and Dad stood up and handed us two envelopes. Mine was purple, and Melody's was a peach color. I carefully opened my envelope to find two checks, one from Mom and one from Dad. The checks totaled two thousand dollars. I was sure Melody had received the same thing, but just to be sure, I looked in her envelope as soon as she set it down.

Mom and Dad said we could use the money for anything we wanted—a used car, college, savings, or whatever. I was thrilled. Just as I was thinking about what I could do with the cash, Mont whispered that he had to go help his mom. He stood and told everyone good-bye, and I walked him outside.

As we walked past the lawn decorations, he reached in his pocket and handed me a long box. I opened it to find a key. Before I could say anything, Mont said, "It's a key to my place." I was speechless. We hugged and leaned against his mom's Lexus. I was overjoyed about receiving the key. Hundreds of thoughts ran through my head as Mont talked. I was officially on cloud nine. When Mont snapped his seat belt, I leaned in and kissed him before he turned the car on.

As Mont drove away, I waved. I couldn't wait to get back inside so I could hook the key onto my key ring. When I turned to go back inside, I glimpsed our mailbox. I wasn't sure whether anyone had gotten the mail today, so I decided to check it. Since I hadn't received a gift from Stanley, he might have sent me a card or something.

Inside the mailbox was a single white envelope addressed to me with no return address. I tore it open with hopes of finding a cash prize. But the envelope contained only a single folded page. Unfolding the paper, I read a sloppily written note that advised me to go get checked out at the health department. Shit! I knew this couldn't be good.

9

I'll Be Damned

The next morning, I woke up early and called the health department. Luckily, someone had just canceled, and I was able to schedule an appointment for ten fifteen. I quickly took a shower and got dressed. When I got to the health department, I parked in the very back because I didn't want anyone to see my car parked here. I flipped the hood of my pullover onto my head and adjusted the strings so that no one could recognize me. Then I walked into the health department and showed the lady at the counter the paper I had received in the mail and told her that I had an appointment.

The lady asked for my identification, and I gave her my driver's license. I guess she was making me a file or something. After the lady had everything she needed from me, she gave me a number and instructed me to have a seat in the waiting room. I sat in the stale-smelling room and thumbed through a birth-control pamphlet until my number was called.

I was greeted by an older nurse who sounded like she had

swallowed a megaphone. She introduced herself and shook my hand as we made our way down the winding hallway. She pointed to an examination room on the left side of the hall, and I ducked in. I had a seat in a chair while she closed the door and proceeded to ask me all sorts of questions about my sex history. She asked me about my sexual preference, how many sexual partners I'd had, whether I participated in oral sex, whether I'd ever had any STDs or abortions, and what type of birth control I used.

I was annoyed that she was talking so loud generally, but when she kept repeating my answers aloud as she made notes in my chart, I finally said something. I didn't know how to tell her to be quiet, so I just asked her if she was deaf. She looked at me like I was crazy and said, "Why, no, darling. I can hear just fine. Why would you ask me a question like that?"

I blushed and whispered, "You are talking really loud, and I think that whoever is in the hallway or in the next room may hear our conversation."

She patted my hand, lowered her voice, and apologized. I let out a huge breath. After telling her about her big mouth, I had to answer only a few more questions before I was left alone to get undressed. I was nervous, but I smelled good. The sweet-pea body butter that I had put on after my shower lingered in the room and gave it a cozy feeling. Just as I was relaxing, the nurse knocked on the door and came in.

She told me to lie back on the examination table and relax. The paper on the table crunched as I lay back and opened my legs. The nurse made small talk about the weather and traffic as she did whatever she had to do to check out my lady parts. The examination didn't take long. She soon told me to put my clothes on and said that she would be back shortly. Within five minutes the nurse was back with bad news.

"What?" I said to the nurse. "I have what?"

The nurse whispered, "Calm down, Ms. Russo. All you have to do is take these pills, and you will be back to normal."

I did exactly what she said. I took the pills for the next couple of days, and the yeast infection and chlamydia cleared up. I never wanted to be in this situation again. I couldn't believe that I had gotten an STD. I had to be more careful. I was so glad that I hadn't had sex with Mont yet.

I promised myself that I would get checked for STDs every six months since I was sexually active. I wondered whether I should tell Stanley since he and I had unprotected sex. *Hell*, I thought, *maybe that's where I got this disease from*. I was officially done with Stanley and Jerry's asses. No more calling, no more cuddling, no more anything.

The next day, Melody found an abortion clinic. She made an appointment for the following week. Since the clinic was a little over an hour away, we told Mom that we were going to a campus tour. She kept asking Melody all of these questions, and Melody just lied her behind off. I never knew she was such a good liar. I swear, I learned something new about her every day.

I figured I would tell Melody the whole health department horror story to get her spirits up before such a serious procedure. We talked, laughed, and even stopped for doughnuts. Melody told me that she wasn't thinking about J.R. anymore because she was going off to college and couldn't be worried about him. I couldn't blame her for that. He seemed to be her weakness, and I knew she didn't want to end up pregnant again.

The clinic was empty and cold inside. Melody signed in, and we sat close to the window. The fat lady behind the counter called Melody up and asked her about the payment. Melody dug in her new Coach bag, fished out four one-hundred-dollar bills, and handed them to the fat lady. The receptionist gave her back what looked like six dollars and some pennies. Melody took the change and the receipt and shoved it down into her purse. Then the fat lady said, "The nurse will be calling you shortly."

As soon as she said that, the nurse popped her head out of a door. Melody looked at me, got up, and went with the nurse wearing the electric-blue scrubs. It seemed like I waited forever before Melody reappeared with the same nurse. The nurse said, "You guys look alike," and handed me some pamphlets and paperwork. I shoved the papers deep down into Melody's purse just like she had done with the change from earlier.

A week later, everything was back to normal. I still hadn't talked to any of my sugar daddies, and I was going to keep it that way. That health department visit had freaked me out. I had been over to Mont's a few times, but I still hadn't used my key. Now that I was all clear of the yeast infection and the chlamydia, I was thinking about trying to seduce Mont. I was going to have to sit him down and tell him I needed sex sometime this week because I was about to burst. I made my mind up: I was going to use the key this week to set the mood.

That night I went by Dana's to pick up a French maid outfit. She had several to choose from, and I couldn't make up my mind. So Dana suggested that I try them on, and she would tell me which one she liked the best. I modeled the all-black outfit and the hot-pink outfit. After I had changed back into my own clothes, Dana asked me to try on the hot-pink one again, so I did. When I came out of the bathroom, she said, "Damn, Mont is so lucky. If I was him, I would be all over you."

I replied, "Your ass is crazy! So you like the pink one the best?"

Dana looked up with a devilish smile and replied, "Yep, that's the one."

After leaving Dana's gated community, I went to the XXX store. I took my sweet time and looked around at all of the freaky things they had to offer. I ended up getting scented votive candles, a huge feather for tickling, and some vanilla body-massage oil with an oil warmer. When I was ready to check out, a tall white guy with black fingernail polish rang me up. He informed me that the condoms in a glass fishbowl by the cash register were buy two, get one free. His suggestive selling technique worked on me. I reached in the bowl and selected three condoms. I was ready to do whatever.

As soon as I got home, I told Melody about my idea of setting the mood at Mont's. "Go for it," she said. "Just don't get pregnant."

That night I was so anxious that I couldn't sleep. I got up at about twelve or so and ran a bubble bath and called Mont. He was lying on his couch watching television when our conversation got a little steamy. I couldn't wait to see what tomorrow had in store for us. I knew that this conversation had worn Mont down by the way he breathed in the phone when I told him that I was pleasuring myself.

10

It's Like That

Today was the big day. I worked my scheduled four hours at Island Getaway, and then I was off to use my key for the first time at Mont's. My overnight bag was packed and in the trunk of the car along with the things I had bought at the XXX store. I couldn't wait to turn that doorknob and have the place to myself for a few hours.

Dinner was in the oven, and votive candles were lit, spreading a sensual aroma throughout the condo. I took a shower and put on the hot-pink French made outfit that Dana adored. It was almost time for Mont to come home, so I ran him a bath. When the bath was ready, I turned on the stereo, and the mood was officially set. Soon after that, I heard Mont's keys in the entry door. I quickly walked down the hall and stood by the door as pretty as a picture.

When Mont walked in, his eyes widened, and so did the smile on his face. Like always, he complimented me on how I looked and kissed me on the cheek. I grabbed his hand and took him to the bathroom. I tried to undress him, but he stopped me and told me that he would take a bath and be out in about fifteen minutes.

"Okay," I said. I didn't let him know I was upset and just went to check on the food.

As I fixed our drinks, Mont came out with a towel wrapped around him.

"Are you ready to eat?" I asked.

He replied, "Yeah." When I reached to get a plate from the cabinet, he said, "I don't need a plate."

I then playfully asked, "How are you going to eat without a plate silly?"

"You're about to see," he said. When I turned around, he dropped his towel. I thought I was going to pass out—because Mont was hung like a horse.

It looked like my wish was finally about to come true. Mont moved in close to me, kissed me, and apologized for making me wait so long. I told him it was okay while I tried to think about what ways would be most comfortable to have sex with him. We made our way to Mont's bedroom, and the wait was over. He started pleasuring me before I could get out of my French maid panties. I was gyrating and moaning all over the bed. I knew I was about to get the big stick soon.

When Mont came up for air, he said, "Turn around." If pleasuring from the front wasn't enough, he also gave me pleasure from the back. I was dripping wet.

I stopped him and said, "We should get a towel because I don't want to get the bed wet." While getting the towel, I dug in the bag from the XXX store and retrieved a condom. When I got back in the bedroom, I handed Mont the condom.

He laughed and said, "You think this is going to fit on me?" He then reached into his drawer beside his bed and pulled out an extra-large condom. He slid the condom onto his erect, thick blessing and whispered,

"I'm about to wear you out." From there we kissed, and he sucked on my neck and nipples. Then Mont got on top and entered me. I had an orgasm immediately because I had wanted him for so long. I had never experienced anything like this. After Mont got into a rhythm, he tore into me like there was no tomorrow. I swear I felt that big thing in my chest. I was screaming and calling his name.

I was almost out of breath when Mont asked if we could switch positions. A minute later, I didn't know what had made me think that I could ride him and that it wouldn't hurt like hell. I was struggling. On my tiptoes, going up and down slowly, I had serious doubts about this position, but I still gave it my all. When I was on top, only half of his blessing was inside of me, until he grasped my waist and gently pulled me down onto him.

I didn't know what to do. I was having all types of orgasms. My love juices were running down my thighs, and I felt so weak. That's when Mont removed his blessing and said, "Are you all right?"

I said, "I think I need a break." I was still straddling him. Even though we weren't connected anymore, I couldn't move. I didn't have the energy.

After I got my strength back, we finished what we'd started. When it was over, I went to the bathroom and sat on the toilet. A little drizzle came out, and it stung. I wiped myself and looked at the tissue—I was bleeding. I couldn't believe Mont had busted my lady parts all up. I had thought I was going to be happy when Mont gave himself to me, but I wasn't. I didn't know what I was going to do with him and that horse dick. It looked like this was going to be a real problem.

When I returned to the bed, Mont's private was still standing tall. "That was a rough ride," I said. He showed compassion and kissed my forehead. I moved the wet towel from the middle of the bed only to unveil another wet spot under that too.

After we changed the sheets, Mont said, "Lyric, I know that I'm a big boy, that's was why I waited so long to have sex with you … I didn't want to scare you off," he said jokingly.

I laughed and said, "I knew it was something, but you having a big ding-a-ling isn't going to scare me away." As I snuggled under his neck, I whispered, "We can have fun practicing." I fell asleep with my head on Mont's toned chest. That was the first night that I stayed with Mont.

Almost a month after Mont unleashed his anaconda on me, I was nearly used to his large blessing. He let me measure it, and it was ten and a half inches long. I learned that I had to give him oral sex for at least ten minutes first. Then we had sex, which didn't last long because Mont was so excited that he couldn't stop himself from climaxing. I could sex him in every position except for riding; that position was still too much for me.

We had sex every day, even when I was on my period. He wasn't scared of a little blood, and besides, I didn't mind. I used to mess with this older guy named Thomas who only liked to sex me when my period was on. I thought it was kind of gross at first, but I got used to it fast because he always gave me whatever my heart desired.

Mont had me spoiled, and I had him spoiled. I officially had a drawer at his house. My Victoria's Secret pajama sets were in there along with a few pairs of lounge pants. I thought I was ready to settle down. I hadn't been thinking about any of my sugar daddies. Mont told me that I didn't have to work, but I still did. Business was really good at Island Getaway. I was saving, hoping I could catch up with Melody's savings.

I finally had decided that I wanted to go to the community college to be a massage technician. When I told Mont, he said, "Seriously, I can get free massages? I think I'm going to like that." As I filled him in about the program, he assured me that he was behind me 100 percent. When I told him about the financial aid, he said that he would pay for it.

Back on Stone Dale Court, it was lonely. Melody was preparing to pack for college, and Mom was going on trips left and right with Desmond. I was nervous as hell about that. Melody told me not to worry, but I still did. On a Thursday, Boogie, Melody, and I went down to Lee Auto Sales. As soon as we got on the lot, I spotted a 2003 black Honda Civic with dark tint and leather interior. I had to have it.

Melody found a red 2005 Maxima, fully loaded. We test-drove a few cars and let the salesman run our credit. We didn't have any, so he told us both that we needed a cosigner. Melody said she might just take our old car with her to Georgia if I had found a car by the middle of August. I told her she might as well load it up because I was going to get that Honda.

After we left the car lot, we swung by the college so I could register for my classes and apply for financial aid. It didn't take long. I was so excited. I was ready to go buy new pens, tablets, and notebooks. After that, we decided to have lunch at Island Getaway. It was busy like always. We sat outside at one of the picnic tables. My friend Sarah was our waitress, and she was flirting her behind off with Boogie. Now that those braces were off, he was really pulling the chicks. It felt good to hang out with these knuckleheads; all that was missing was Raquel.

11

What a Day

The next day I decided to deposit some of my tips from Island Getaway in the bank. My savings account was growing, and I was tempted to go make an offer on that Honda. I fought the urge and decided to wait a little longer. I was off work, so I swung by the mall to see if there were any good sales. Whenever I went to the mall, I always went in through the food court. I felt like I could be seen by everybody there; I wanted everybody to know that I had arrived. My makeup was right, and I was dressed to impress, like always.

The smell of the food hit me dead in the face when I walked into the mall. I decided to get something light to eat on the way out. At that moment I was on a mission. Guess had sexy tight T-shirts on sale for 19.99, so I picked up a red one. I also found a cute strapless dress on clearance for forty bucks. I figured I'd better get out of there so that I would have some money to spend at another store. I was passing the Gap when I remembered I had received a hundred-dollar Gap gift card for a graduation gift.

When I walked into the store, I saw some colorful tank tops on a table. I ended up getting one of every color since they were so cheap. I looked around the store one last time before getting in line and saw a girl who looked like Dana. She was checking out the swimsuits. When I walked over, I caught her eye, and she looked at me. It was my thieving buddy.

She said, "Hey, pretty brown."

I replied, "Hey, birthday girl. How does it finally feel to be nineteen?"

"The same, I guess."

I smiled and said, "Tell me about it. So what are you up to today?"

"Not much. About to go grab some lunch and then go back home, I guess," Dana said.

I replied, "I have to get something to eat too. My stomach is starting to burn."

Dana let out a laugh and suggested that we have lunch together.

We agreed that we didn't want to eat at the food court. So we went down the road to an Olive Garden. Before we got out of the car at the restaurant, Dana said, "I'm buying your lunch today."

I mumbled, "But it's your birthday. I should pay for you."

Dana acted like she didn't hear me. When I got to the door, she held the door open for me. She was acting really weird.

The hostess showed us to our booth and scooted off quickly. We ordered some waters with lemon and looked over the menu. I noticed that when I talked to Dana, she looked dead in my eyes. I also caught her looking at my cleavage a couple of times. I wondered what was up with her, especially when she grabbed my hand.

I snatched my hand away and said, "Dana what are you doing?"

"I'm sorry," she said, putting her head down on the glossy table and taking a deep breath. With that same breath of air, she said, "Lyric, I have a crush on you."

I damn near choked on my breadstick.

"I've been crushing on you since the ninth grade," Dana said.

I sputtered out, "Why now? What made you say something?"

Dana explained that the modeling of the French maid outfits had made her think some pretty nasty thoughts about me. She admitted that she couldn't stop thinking about me and had even had a dream about me. I was blown away.

"I'm sorry," she said. "I shouldn't have said anything."

I replied, "It's okay. We are still cool."

During the rest of our lunch, she looked pretty bummed. I nonchalantly changed the subject by ogling and commenting on the food that the waiter took to the table beside us.

When we left the restaurant, Dana said, "I need to make a quick stop by my house. I need to get the stolen merchandise out of my car before we go back to the mall."

"That's fine," I said as I fastened my seat belt.

When we walked into her bedroom, it was dark. Dana hit the light switch on the wall and said, "Do you want to see the new things I picked up?"

I smiled and replied, "Why not?"

"Do you want something to drink?" she asked.

"Do you have any liquor?"

"Of course," she said, "but it's in the main house. Whatever you want, I could mix it up for you."

I put in an order for something sweet and fruity. In less than five minutes, Dana returned with a drink garnished with cherries and a lime on the rim of the funky-shaped glass. She then handed me a straw and started sorting through the assortment of stolen goods.

While I sat on the edge of the bed and sipped my drink, Dana bragged about how easy it had been to take the things she had stolen over the past couple of weeks. She was talking, but I wasn't listening. I couldn't believe that Dana was sweet on me. She was attractive, and I wondered if she had ever been with any chicks.

Before I knew it, I had finished my drink, and I asked for another. Dana gave me a refill without hesitation. Not long after I finished half of my second drink, I started feeling really hot, and I told Dana I needed to lie down. I headed for the couch, but she insisted that I make myself at home on her queen-size bed.

I had never been big on drinking, and I might have had a little too much. I took off my shoes and basically passed out the minute my head hit the Ralph Lauren pillows. I had a crazy dream that Dana was kissing my neck and rubbing me all over with some kind of oil. It didn't seem like I was asleep long, but when I came to, it was almost three o'clock. I popped up like a Pop-Tart fresh out of the toaster and said, "What happened?"

"I think you drank too fast and passed out," she replied.

I wanted that to be the whole truth, but I knew something had happened because of the sweet smell and residue of oil on my skin. Back at the mall, Dana parked and walked me to my car. She said, "Are you okay to drive yourself home?"

"Yes," I replied as she opened my car door. As I backed out of the parking space, she watched me with those killer green eyes.

At the red light, I flipped the mirror on the visor open to put some gloss on my lips. Immediately, my eyes were drawn to a dime-sized hickey on my neck. I called Dana and said, "What did you do to me?"

She giggled and replied, "I couldn't resist stealing a little bit of sugar off of you while you were resting."

I was speechless. Dana had talked her slick talk and gotten away with seducing me without my consent. Without saying good-bye or "talk to you later," I ended the call by hanging up. I couldn't believe this girl who had always been a great friend to me was checking me out. I tried to calculate how many times she purposely had seen me naked or brushed up against me. I felt sick because this was a side of Dana I had never seen, and I thought I liked it.

12

She's Leaving

The week before Melody had to leave for college had finally come. We were shopping for everything from laptops to twin-size bedding. We went to World Market and found some neat artwork to hang on her walls. Melody ended up getting most of her dorm stuff from there and from Target. I couldn't wait to see pictures of her dorm room after she got everything put together.

Mom had cosigned for Melody to get that Maxima. I still hadn't made up my mind about the Honda. I figured I would keep saving while driving the slate-gray 1998 Camry that Melody and I had shared since the tenth grade. Nothing was wrong with it, and it was paid for. I had a new way of thinking since I was considering getting my own apartment. I had thought about asking Mont if I could move in permanently, but I didn't want to crowd him. Plus, I didn't think it was healthy for such a new relationship.

⚯

At the crack of dawn, we hugged, cried, kissed, and went back in the house over twenty times to make sure my mirror image hadn't forgotten anything. The Maxima was jam-packed with plastic bins, suitcases, books, hangers, and pillows. I wondered if someone would help Melody get all of this stuff out of her car at her dorm. I hoped that her roommates would be clean and considerate. If they weren't, I knew that I would be hearing all about it.

As we watched Melody drive off, Mom, Boogie, and I waved. We didn't care that Melody was half a mile down the road and couldn't see us anymore. I looked a mess. I was crying like I would never see her again. Mom rubbed my back and told me not to worry because Melody was coming back for Thanksgiving and Christmas. As soon as she said that, my phone rang.

I pulled myself together to answer my phone. It was Melody calling me from her new cell phone. We ended up talking for the next four hours. She told me how much she was going to miss me and how nervous she was about meeting her roommates. I told her not to worry and that things would go well. After I got off the phone with Melody, I took a quick shower and got ready for work. I knew it was going to be busy today because it was so hot.

Like I had guessed, work was busy and went by super-fast. I made over seventy bucks in tips, and two guys asked for my phone number. I took their numbers and told them that I might call. Mont had left a message on my phone asking if I wanted to stay at his place that night. I called and declined because I missed my sister so much that I was going to sleep in her bed tonight.

The next few weeks were pretty fair, and I found myself home alone multiple times while Mom went on so-called business trips with Desmond. Mont stayed over one night. We watched a few movies and talked over bowls of cereal. I admitted that I was kind of depressed about Melody being gone. He told me that he had known something was wrong because I hadn't been acting like myself.

I was getting ready to tell him about my suspicions about my mom and his dad when my phone vibrated on the countertop. Mont kissed me on the nape of my neck as he got up to put his cereal bowl in the sink. I answered without looking to see who it was as I smiled at Mont. It was Stanley. I quickly said, "I'm going to have to call you back, girl. Now isn't a good time," and ended the phone call. I decided not to kill the vibe by telling Mont that we might end up being stepsiblings. As I continued to crunch on my cereal, Mont rubbed my back. After I was done eating, I took Mont's hand and led him upstairs to Mom's shower. I decided that we would take a nice hot shower and that he would stay with me on Stone Dale Court tonight.

The shower revived me. The hot water got my blood pumping, and Mont made me horny as he washed my hot spots. As much as I tried, I could not stop thinking about Dana touching me and how good it must have felt to my unresponsive body. I wished I had been alert to experience my first lesbian love session. That night I realized I wanted to be with Dana again, but this time I wanted to be fully aware of what was going on.

The sex was so damn good. When Mont tasted me, all I could think about was Dana doing me the same way. I wanted him to go deeper and deeper. It seemed like I couldn't get enough. That night I took Mont's large blessing and was looking for more. Thinking about Dana while having sex with Mont had me on fire. My full-size bed squeaked while I rode him like a runaway horse. After Mont climaxed, he fell asleep in no time. Meanwhile, I lay awake as thoughts of Dana danced in my head.

13

Someone Pinch Me

Lately, I was hanging with Dana just about every day that I didn't go to work. She was real touchy-feely, whispering in my ear and even tickling me. I didn't tell her to stop; she knew I didn't mind. Ever since I'd let her slide on giving me that hickey, she had been affectionate. I had to admit, I loved spending time with her.

Mont was working with his dad now, and he was going out of town a lot too. I started to wonder if he had someone else on the side. I honestly didn't know where this relationship was going. It felt like we were kind of drifting apart. We were spending less and less time together. I didn't know how I would deal with it if he was cheating. I sure hoped he wasn't.

Mom was busy as ever working and working out. She got a gym membership, and she stayed at that place when she wasn't out of town with Desmond. Mom and Mrs. Coco were both classy ladies, but my mom was in shape and was prettier than Mrs. Coco. They were almost the same brown color, but Mrs. Coco was thick, too thick. I could tell she wore girdles under her designer clothes because I could see the lines. My mom didn't need any girdles; her shit was tight.

Melody was enjoying school, and so far she liked all three of her roommates. One was a geek, one was a prep, and the other was a free spirit. She sent me pictures of her room the same week she arrived, and she did a good job decorating it. I couldn't wait to visit Melody and meet all of her roomies. That would be much later, though. Maybe spring break.

Boogie was going to the same college where I was about to start. He was studying to be a physical therapist's assistant. He was dating a girl who worked with me at Island Getaway, and they made a cute couple. I hoped that Boogie would do her right, but I knew how Boogie was. He would probably end up meeting a new chick on campus. God knows he changed girlfriends like he changed his socks.

When I checked my e-mail the Friday before start of the semester, I was shocked to find out that I had to pay for all of my books. That came up to a grand total of four hundred bucks. My classes started on Tuesday, and financial aid covered all of my classes, but that was it. Even though I had been saving, I decided that I was going to ask Mont for the money. He had said he would help me if I needed him to.

That night I told Mont that I was going to stay home, but I changed my mind. On the drive over to his place, I called Dana to talk to her about the school situation. I told her that I was nervous about touching strangers. Dana laughed and told me I could practice my massage techniques on her. I said that I would think about it. As I parked in front of Mont's condo, I ended the call with Dana.

When I unlocked the door to Mont's place, it was dark. A few candles were burning, and Ja Rule was playing on the stereo. As I made my way back toward the bedroom, I heard the shower running. I decided to surprise Mont and jump in the shower with him. I took my clothes off, left them in a pile on the floor, and quietly opened the bathroom door. Steam escaped past me with the pleasant aroma of Zest. The lights were on a dim setting, and the steam had the bathroom so foggy that I could hardly see.

When I finally made my way to the shower entrance and walked in, I could have sworn that my eyes were deceiving me, but they weren't. There was a silhouette that was as shapely as my own, but shorter. Even though I knew this couldn't be Mont, I quickly called out his name, and the voice screamed, "What the hell?"

"W-what?" I stuttered. As I ran out of the shower, I slid on the floor toward the wall where the light switch was. The shape that confronted me was all hips and ass with boobs the size of the ones I had in the third grade. The stranger's skin was wet and pasty; she needed some sun or a tanning bed ASAP. She wore a short weave that was different shades of blonde. I counted at least four tattoos and noticed a small gap in her teeth as she fussed at me.

After I grabbed a towel and covered myself, I stormed out of the bathroom. The stranger was on my heels. I yelled, "Who are you, and what are you doing in my man's shower?"

She yelled back, "Mont is my man!"

I sure as hell didn't believe that. I couldn't believe this whole situation. This was like a bad dream. All I could do was sit on the edge of Mont's bed and put my head in my hands.

Before I could ask her anything, she started giving me all kinds of information that I wasn't even sure I wanted. The wet bitch's name was Latria. She told me that she'd met Mont at a gas station about two months ago. She knew all about Mont's birthmark and about his anaconda. I was speechless. My mouth was dry, and I felt like throwing up. All I could do was sit there and shake my head. I got my phone out of my purse and called Mont. He didn't answer.

Latria smirked and said, "Watch this." She pulled out her phone and put it on speaker as she dialed Mont's number.

That asshole answered on the first ring. "I'm on my way, baby," he said. "I hope you're wet already."

I quickly said, "Yeah, she's wet all right."

When he heard my voice, he tried to explain, but Latria hung up. I had heard enough. I told her that she could have him and that I was leaving. I slipped on my clothes, not even bothering to dry off. I gathered my things out of my drawer while, surprisingly, Latria tried to comfort me. The whole time, she was naked and seemed very comfortable that way. I was beyond hurt, but I couldn't cry on her shoulder.

On my way out of the apartment, Latria asked if I could give her a ride to her house about twenty minutes away. My lips moved before I could think properly, and I told her yes. After quickly gathering her things out of the bathroom. Latria put on a shirt, some of Mont's jogging pants and some flip-flops, and we both got the hell out of there. After we got in the car, I started to change my mind about giving her a ride, but she was already adjusting the passenger seat and putting on her seat belt. Down the road, I had to stop at a store and park because I couldn't stop crying and thinking about how Mont could have done this. I hated him for making me feel so crappy. I was so mad that I wanted to snatch his balls off.

After handing me some Kleenex out of her purse, Latria sat still and apologized. She claimed that she hadn't known about me. I told her that it was okay and that Mont was going to get what he deserved for this. I managed to pull myself together because I didn't want her to think I was a water barrel. It took everything I had in me not to stop again and break down. When we finally made it to Latria's place, she insisted I come in and have a cup of hot tea to calm my nerves. Once we were inside the small but cozy apartment, Latria didn't have to show me around; I could see everything except her bathroom and bedroom from where I was sitting. The walls were different shades of tan, and for furniture, there was only a plum-colored couch and a television on a rickety stand. That was it.

She offered me something to drink other than the coffee she was about to prepare, and I asked for a shot of anything she had. We both swallowed two shots of cheap liquor along with the coffee, as we sat on the couch and started talking. I learned so many things about Latria that night. She was a twin also; her mirror image was a boy. She was a year older than I was, and I wondered why I had never seen her around here before. We talked and talked until I ended up falling asleep.

When I woke up, there was a tattered quilt over me. I smelled French toast and sausage cooking. Latria had made breakfast for the both of us. I wasn't expecting that at all. Hell, I didn't even know how I'd ended up sleeping over at this stranger's house. After I washed my face, I joined Latria at the table, where she sat wearing a worn, faded head scarf. That's when I noticed she had freckles, lots of them. I hadn't noticed them last night. Maybe it was too dark, or maybe I was just too upset to notice or even care. After I drank a glass of milk, we exchanged numbers, and I had a new friend in a neighboring city.

14

All These Ladies

The night before school started, Dana cooked for me, so I went over to her place at about five o'clock. I knew this would keep me from thinking about Mont. She made some kind of angel hair pasta with blackened lamb chops, and it was delicious. It was the perfect way to end such a wicked weekend. We decided to watch the movie *Crash* after dinner. I took one end of the couch, and Dana took the other, but by the time the previews were over, she had inched her way behind me and put her hand across my hip. I didn't say anything. I just smiled.

Dana had me so hot that I knew there was a wet spot in the crotch of my thong. She kissed my neck, ears, and shoulders. It felt so good. I wanted to go all the way with her, but I hadn't shaved in two days, plus I didn't want to stay out too late because I had school in the morning. I did kiss her on the lips and told her we could do something real soon. That made Dana's face light up. I could tell she was falling for me.

I didn't tell Dana about the whole Mont and Latria situation. I didn't want her to be worried about me. Mont had left over twenty messages on my phone. I deleted them without even listening to them and didn't return any of his calls. I ended up buying my books with the money I had saved up.

The first day of school was interesting. I sat in the front of my classes so that I wouldn't get distracted. I could have sat at the back, though, because I was the only interesting-looking person in most of the classes. When I got out of my last class, I was thirsty, so I went by the vending machine to get a drink. As I dug for some change in my bag, my bangles chimed away. I fished out three quarters and put them into the machine. After popping the top on my soda, I started towards my car. I hadn't found a good parking spot that morning, so I had to walk a bit.

When I got out toward the end of the parking lot, I noticed a truck just like Stanley's near my car. I walked slowly, hoping that it wasn't him, but when the door opened on the dark green Silverado, a loafer stepped out, and I knew that it was Stanley.

"My sweet Lyric, I've been calling you. Why haven't you returned any of my calls?" he said as he reached out for a hug.

I replied, "I met someone."

Stanley's face looked like he had just sucked on a lemon when he heard the news. "I miss you. My wife isn't satisfying me," he said.

"Let me think about it, Stanley," I said as I let him go.

He must have been happy with that because he pulled out a wad of cash and gave it to me. "Go buy yourself something pretty," he said as he got in his truck and pulled away. I meant to ask him how he'd known where I was, but it was too late now because he had already left.

After I got in my car, I pulled the bills apart and started to count. Stanley had given me a little over seven hundred bucks. I couldn't believe it. I needed retail therapy more than ever now, but I stopped by the bank and deposited four hundred dollars first. It was almost three o'clock, and I figured the mall would be empty, but I was wrong. I promised myself

I wouldn't stay at the mall long because Mom was coming back today. I wanted to do something really nice for her, and I was thinking about cooking her favorite meal.

The first stop I made was at a specialty scarf store. They had scarves in all different colors and materials, and I dropped thirty-six bucks on a scarf for Latria's weave. It was black with different colored splashes. I then bought Dana a green polo shirt to match her eyes, and that was it. I didn't buy anything for myself. This was the quickest I had ever been in and out of the mall.

The leather in the car burned my back as I sat down. It was a terrible day to have worn a tank top, I thought, as I felt for blisters. I decided to let the air pump out for a minute while I cooled off. I looked around at all of the people in the parking lot. There were old couples walking hand in hand, new mothers with strollers, men with their homeboys, and women fighting with the wind to keep their dresses down.

Just as I was thinking about why people flock to the mall and about the idea of retail therapy, I saw a familiar face. It was Raquel and some guy with a fade. *Oh my goodness*, I thought. *What is Raquel doing with this cutie?* Before I knew it, I blew the horn and waved for Raquel to come over.

When Raquel got closer, I noticed that she had stepped her game up. She looked cute dressed in Guess from head to toe. Her hair was braided in some elaborate design, and she wore just enough lip gloss to attract attention to her lips. Raquel said, "You just getting here, or you about to leave?"

I replied, "About to leave," as I adjusted the air.

"Oh, my bad," said Raquel. "This is my godsister, Alexis."

Godsister? Where at? I thought. All I saw was the dude behind her. My thoughts were interrupted when Raquel's companion stepped forward and said, "You can call me Alex, pretty lady."

If I weren't already sitting down, I would have fallen back. Alexis—or Alex—was a girl who dressed like a guy. Her sagging shorts and big shirt had fooled me. Raquel's godsister was a stud.

After I added two plus two in my head and got the facts straight, Raquel and I carried on a conversation about what we were doing now and who went where for college. But I wasn't really focusing on Raquel; I was glancing over her shoulder, looking at Alexis. She was so fine. She had light brown skin and hazel eyes, and her accent was very attractive; she had to be from Jersey or New York. She looked to be about 5'5". I wanted to know more about Alex. So I decided I would go back inside the mall with them.

It didn't take long for Alex to start hitting on me. I couldn't believe she was so damn cute. When she smiled, I noticed how deep her dimples were. I ended up spending a hundred more bucks on shirts and smell-good junk. On the way back to the car, I tried to give Raquel my phone number, but she was on her phone. So I just gave it to Alex and jumped back into the hot seat once again.

15

Afternoon Quickie

Two months into school, things were looking good. I was studying and giving all my buddies equal attention. I had learned that Alex was a player and decided that I wasn't going to be anything but a friend to her. I knew that she had been with a lot of girls, and I didn't want to end up back at the clinic again. We only talked on the phone and hung out a little. I still hadn't returned any of Mont's phone calls. He was a basket case without me. He left cards on the windshield of my car and flowers at my doorstep. I had to admit, I got kind of soft and listened to some of his voice mail messages, but I still wasn't ready to talk to him.

I talked to Latria on the phone every day, and things were real cool between us. She invited me over for lunch and a movie on a Saturday. I was kind of excited because I hadn't seen her since that first time I'd accidentally stayed over at her apartment. When I got to her apartment, I primped in the mirror before I walked to the door. Just as I was about to knock, Latria opened the door with a towel wrapped around her and said, "Come on in. Have a seat."

I sat down in the living room on that same plum couch. The smell of yams and pork chop danced around me. I was ready to eat but couldn't get my mind off of her in that towel. When she returned, the old head rag was off, and a new sassy do was unveiled. She wore a white tank top and some tight black jogging shorts with the word "kiss" across the ass.

Latria said, "Well, damn, can I get a hug? I haven't seen you for a while." As she hugged me, I realized her neck smelled sweeter that those yams did. After the hug, she invited me into the kitchen. I stood there and watched as she fished the meat out of the deep fryer and let it soak on some napkins on a plate. I made small talk and thanked her for inviting me while she started to fix our plates. She smiled and said, "I missed those pretty eyes of yours. I had to see them again."

I blushed and took the plate she handed to me. I sat down at the two-person dining table and thought about her scarf in the car. Latria finally sat her plump ass down in the chair in front of me. While we ate, she told me about this crazy customer she had at the DMV. I laughed because I knew that she had wanted to tell the old man to go to hell.

After we finished eating, I got up to wash the dishes, but she wouldn't let me. As she started washing them, I said, "I will be right back. I left something in the car." I walked out to the car, retrieved the bag, and returned to the kitchen. Latria was almost finished washing the dishes when I sat down at the table. She hit me with the drying rag as she was about to exit the kitchen and said, "Come on, let's go watch some TV."

I got up and headed toward the couch. When I sat down, she said, "Why are you sitting there? Come on, we're going to watch the movie in my bedroom."

I got up, grabbed the gift bag, and replied, "Oh, okay." I followed her to the bedroom. The walls in her room were black, to my surprise. The carpet was an off-white color, and zebra-print bedding was on her bed. There was a huge entertainment system around a big-screen TV. I was shocked at how large her bedroom was compared to the rest of the apartment.

"What are you holding?" Latria asked.

I handed her the bag and said, "It's just a little something for you."

She took the bag, opened it, and pulled out the scarf. Latria yelled, "Aw, this is just darling! That was so nice of you." She kissed me on the cheek and started dancing around with her new scarf. She said, "I'm going to throw away my old scarf right now."

I laughed, sat on the foot of the bed, and waited for her to return from the bathroom.

She returned quickly because the movie was about to start. I still didn't know what we were watching until I saw a scene with three naked girls dancing. I said, "We're watching porn? Are you serious?"

Latria looked at me and said, "As a heart attack."

I just sat there with my mouth open. I couldn't believe this. After about ten minutes, Latria got up and took off her jogging shorts. She then asked me if I could massage her pleasure zone. I choked up because I had never touched another female like that.

I did what she asked even though I was out of my element. I didn't know what I was doing, but Latria was making all kinds of noises. My fingers were really slippery, and I was starting to get hot myself. Shortly after this game started, it got even more interesting: Latria reached in her drawer and pulled out the blackest, biggest dildo I had ever seen. She inserted the tip into her wet opening and aggressively shoved it in. I looked at her, and she smiled. She then took my hand and put it on the end of the toy. My bangles jingled as I pulled my hand back and forth, over and over again, until she let out a loud "Ahhhhh."

I couldn't believe what I had participated in. I was fully clothed, but I felt naked. Latria looked at me and said, "Thanks, Lyric. I needed that." I didn't say anything. I got up, went to the bathroom, and closed the door. While in the bathroom, I stared at myself in the mirror. I had an urge to smell my fingers, but I didn't. I quickly washed my hands and wet a clean washcloth to cool down my face. When I came out of the bathroom, Latria had her shorts on and had turned the TV to TBS like nothing had happened.

Before I left Latria's apartment, she fixed me a plate to go and kissed me on my cheek again. As soon as I started driving, my phone rang. It was Dana's ringtone. I answered, and she asked if I could come over for dinner around six. I told her I couldn't wait to see her, and I would be there. It was almost two o'clock. I had time to go home and get fresh. I was ready for her after what had just happened with Latria and me.

16

She Lust Me

When I got home, there was a card and a box in the screen door. I scooped them up and went upstairs. I put the card and box on the dresser and took a cool ten-minute shower. While wrapped in a towel, I opened the card with damp hands: another "I'm sorry" from Mont. I threw it in the trash. I ripped open the box to find three shiny gold bangles. The inside of each bangle was engraved. One read "Mont," another read "loves," and the last one read "Lyric."

I thought, *Maybe it's time to have a sit-down with him. It has been about two months. Maybe tomorrow I'll call him. Yes, I will call him tomorrow.* Sitting down on my bed, I rubbed body butter all over myself. I then added the three new bangles to the existing eight bangles on my left arm. My bangles chanted a nervous jingle as I put on a black sexy panty set.

I thought about what had just happened with Latria, and I started to blush. The cool shower hadn't helped me at all. I was still on fire from the events that had taken place at Latria's apartment. With naughty thoughts dancing in my head, I threw on some jogging pants and a tank top, and I was out of the door just as fast as I had come in.

∽∞∼

Inside Dana's love den it smelled wonderful, only I wasn't really that hungry because of the big lunch I'd had with Latria. Dana smiled as I walked through the door, but when she noticed that I was carrying a gift bag, she looked confused. I handed the bag to her and planted a soft kiss on her cheek. She turned beet-red and then moved the tissue paper around and pulled out the polo shirt. Before I could say anything, Dana was on me like white on rice. She planted a kiss on me that I wouldn't forget anytime soon.

"Thank you, pretty brown," she said as she smacked me on the ass and then walked away to check the oven. I stood there kind of dazed. I was ready to drop my jogging pants for her, and I had just walked in. I knew that tonight was going to be unforgettable.

Dinner was delicious. From there things only got better. Dana instructed me to lie down on her bed, and I did. After I lay down, she slowly removed my jogging pants and tank top while placing the softest kisses on my skin. Next, she fed me strawberries dipped into chocolate and licked the chocolate off of my lips. After she licked my lips, she tongue-kissed me. There was so much passion in her kiss that I let my shyness go and kissed her back. It felt like she was hungry for me; we were hungry for each other.

I loved this. It felt so good, and she turned me on. I pushed her off of me and straddled her. We kissed and licked each other's necks. I was so wet I couldn't stand it. Before I knew it, I was out of those little black panties and calling out for God. That girl worked me over real good. I couldn't believe that I was actually satisfied without a penis.

There were hickeys all over Dana's neck by the end, and even though we were done, I still wanted her on me, teasing me with her tongue, lips, and fingers. After the lust session was finished, we talked over what was left of the strawberries. I told her that Mont and I had had a falling out and that I hadn't been talking to him. Of course, she wanted more details, but I told her only the minimum. On the sly I changed the subject and started teasing her with the strawberries. That led to an X-rated hot shower together and a long steamy night of grinding and pure pleasure.

Waking up to breakfast in bed was fantastic. Dana made me French toast, bacon, and sunny-side-up cheesy eggs. She was a beast in the kitchen. I never knew Dana could cook like that. I could get used to waking up to that great aroma and those gorgeous green eyes. I couldn't believe that one day with Latria and one night with Dana had me thinking about leaving penis alone. Wait, was I really thinking that? Maybe I wasn't sane right now. Maybe Dana had put a love spell on me.

If Dana had put a love spell on me, it didn't last long because as soon as I made that right turn out of the gated community, I called Latria. We laughed and talked all the way to my house. Neither one of us brought up what had happened the day before. I decided that I wouldn't say anything and would just see what happened the next time we got together. I ended the call with Latria as I lay back on my bed.

I could barely keep my eyes open. Dana and I had stayed up late and had gotten hardly any sleep. I napped for almost two hours before my cell phone rang and woke me up. I looked at the screen and saw that it was Mr. King Ding-a-Ling himself. I decided to finally answer his phone call. Mont expressed how happy he was to hear my voice. It didn't take long for him to ask if he could come by and see me. I told him that would be fine.

I didn't primp or even brush my teeth. I just went outside and sat on the steps with my flat hair and the sleep lines on my face. I wasn't dressed to impress—in fact, I had on the same jogging pants and T-shirt from the night before. It wasn't long before I saw a cherry-red H2 making its way down Stone Dale Court. The massive SUV took up the remainder of the driveway.

I couldn't see Mont through the dark tint. However, I knew it was him because the car had a Coco's Creations tag on the front that resembled the Chanel emblem. He climbed out of the H2 with a dozen roses just as red as the SUV. I took the flowers and let Mont hug me. I hugged him back with one arm. I couldn't lie—his arms felt really good. We ended up going inside so I could put the flowers in some water.

We sat at the counter, and I listened to everything he had to say. He told me that he loved me and that he'd had a weak moment. He begged me to forgive him and said he even wanted me to move in with him. I told him that I had trust issues with him, and I couldn't make a decision so soon, considering that I had found a naked girl in his shower. I did tell him that we could be friends until I made my decision. He accepted what I told him, and I gave him his key back.

Mont then asked for a hug. As he hugged me he, caressed my back. His hands went lower and lower. Before I knew it, it he was massaging my behind. He smelled so damn good. Then the hug turned into a kiss. The next thing I knew, my pants were off, and his pants were down around his expensive designer sneakers. Soon we were having sex up against the wall like there was going to be no tomorrow. I couldn't believe that a hug had led to this. I'd had no intentions of having sex with Mont after he cheated on me and broke my heart.

After giving up my goodies unintentionally, I did the walk of shame and cleaned myself up in our downstairs bathroom. I slipped my jogging pants back on and told Mont that it was time for him to go. He tried to hug me again, but this time I resisted. I walked him out to his H2 and complimented him on how nice it was. He told me that I could ride in it anytime. I nodded my head and said okay.

Mont then asked if he could take me out or come back and visit me tomorrow or next weekend. I told him I didn't think that would be a good idea. Even though we'd just had some pretty amazing sex, he looked bummed out. While he backed his new humongous SUV out of the driveway, I turned, walked up the steps, and went into the house. I didn't look back. It wasn't my fault that he had messed up a good thing.

17

He Did What

The next week flew by, and Friday was back before I knew it. I had to work from four until twelve at Island Getaway. It was almost one in the morning when we locked up the restaurant and walked to our cars. I was thinking about Dana when I started the engine. Just then my phone rang; it was Latria. As soon as I answered, I could tell that she had been crying or was about to cry. She was trying to talk, but the words never made it out; her hysterical sobbing forced me to make a U-turn in the road.

When I got to Latria's apartment, I knocked on the door. She opened it quickly. "He's gone, Lyric!" she cried. "He's gone. My brother is dead!"

My heart sank down into my freshly painted toes. I thought back to the night I had met Latria. She had told me how proud she was of her brother and that he was in the military. She had even shown me pictures of him and his wife, who had just had a baby.

I couldn't believe it. Her mirror image was gone. Latria was a wreck. All I could do was hug her. I noticed that her face was hot and that she had pissed herself. I tried to get her to calm down, but it wasn't working. She started throwing up and wouldn't stop crying. I decided to run her a shower and try to get her cleaned up a little bit. By this time the tears had stopped, but the moans were still present. I managed to get her out of her clothes and in the warm shower, but she wouldn't even stand up. I lathered her up with body wash and let the shower rinse it away.

I gave her a towel to dry off with and told her to put on her pink nightshirt that was hanging on the back of the bathroom door. Meanwhile, I looked in the medicine cabinet for some Tylenol for me and for her. I walked Latria to her bed and handed her a glass of water and the Tylenol. She took it, balled up in the fetal position, and clutched a pillow. My clothes were soaked with water from helping her in the shower, so I peeled off my wet Island Getaway uniform and put on one of Latria's oversized nightshirts. I then got a throw blanket to cover us up, turned out the light, and lay behind Latria and rubbed her back. The snorting didn't last too much longer. After a few minutes, she was out cold.

I woke to the sun in my face. I hadn't noticed that the blinds were open last night when I tucked Latria in. It was early, a little after eight. I decided to make her a light breakfast, some oatmeal, toast, and eggs. When I was done in the kitchen, I shook her gently, and her bloodshot eyes fluttered. Tear stains were still fresh on her pale face. I said, "I made you a little something."

Latria replied, "I don't have much of an appetite."

Before I could reply to Latria, her phone rang. She tried to answer, but the person on the other end of the line couldn't hear her, so I took the phone and said hello. It was Latria's mom, and her voice sounded dry and raspy too. I introduced myself and filled her in on Latria's well-being. I told her that I was trying to get Latria to eat a little and that she was hoarse from crying and yelling. Her mother told me that she knew Latria was going to take it hard. I couldn't imagine it because I too was a twin. Latria's mom thanked me for being there for her child at her time of need. She explained that she was driving and would reach Latria's apartment within the hour. She then sent her love through the phone to Latria and told her to stay strong.

After the conversation with Latria's mom, I sat with Latria for another thirty minutes before I asked her if she would be okay until her mom got here. She let out a soft "yes." I then gave her a hug and told her that I would be back to check on her. Before I let myself out, I closed the blinds in her bedroom and locked the bottom lock on the front door.

When I pulled in my driveway, I noticed that Mont's shiny H2 was parked by the curb. That seemed fitting, considering that's where I had kicked him. I figured he was there to beg, so I took my time getting out of the car. I was thinking about Latria and hoping that she would be okay; I really did feel sorry for her.

As I stuck my key in the door and turned the knob, I was deep in thought. All of a sudden, I was pushed forward with so much force that I fell to my knees. I looked back to see Mont's enraged face. As I struggled to grab hold of the counter, potpourri and my mom's candles hit the floor. Mont was ranting and raving about how he had seen my car at Latria's house late last night. I didn't have a chance to say anything. Mont yelled, "I saw you and her in the bed, Lyric! I saw the both of you through the window. You are such a whore!"

I couldn't believe what was happening. As I got up off of the floor, I made my way to the counter and threw a glass candle at Mont. It missed and smashed against the wall beside him. That must have brought Mont back to reality because he then immediately ran over to me and tried to hug me. I pushed him off of me and told him to leave before I called the cops. With his cowardly head hung low, he left, and I slammed the door behind him.

I took a deep breath and looked at the mess I was left to clean up. I got the broom and cleaned up all traces of the potpourri, glass, and wax. I put the stools back at the counter and made a mental note to replace Mom's candle on my next trip to the mall. Last but not least, I pulled my pants down to see if my knees were bruised from being pushed down. They were turning purple already.

I wanted to call Latria, but I knew that now wasn't a good time, so I called Melody and filled her in on everything that had happened with Latria and Mont. She couldn't believe her ears—especially when I told her that I had to cut our conversation short because I had a date with Stanley at Morgan's Towers in the next town over.

18

No Way, José

When I got to the hotel, it was way more than I had expected. It was something like I had seen on TV. In the lobby there was a wall of glass, and I could see all of the nice landscaping around the property. I got on the elevator and pushed the button to go to the tenth floor. Some jazzy music kept me company on the way up. I reached the room that Stanley had reserved, put on a fake smile, and knocked on the door.

Stanley opened the door wearing a plush robe and a smile. I smiled back as I entered the room, and he took my bag and set it on the bed. I looked around and had to admit that it was the nicest hotel that I had ever been in. He then took my hand and led me to the bathroom. The Jacuzzi had a waterfall faucet that was already pouring gallons of hot water into the tub. The mirror was covered in steam, the lights were off, and small votive candles were lit.

Stanley helped me out of my shirt and unsnapped my bra; I shimmied out of my jeans all by myself and quickly got in the Jacuzzi so that Stanley wouldn't see the bruises on my knees. He slipped out of his robe and was in the tub in no time, nappy chest hairs and all. As soon as Stanley got in the tub, the conversation began. He told me that he missed me and that he wanted to hold me, so I maneuvered myself in between his hairy legs and rested my back on his chest.

"Lyric, I'm leaving my wife. I want us to be together."

It was a good thing that I was sitting down because that announcement made me weak. I immediately asked him if he was serious.

Stanley replied, "Yes." His voice was so firm, like I had already said okay. Stanley said, "I want to wake up with you every morning. My wife is dull, and she can't satisfy me like you do."

I was really blown away. I didn't know what to say, so I didn't say anything just yet.

The bubble bath finished me off. Afterward, I didn't want lunch or sex. I wanted a long nap. After working last night, and then spending this morning with Latria, I was exhausted. I didn't feel like doing anything other than sleep, but Stanley was wide awake and erect. I knew he was ready to play. I lay down on the bed and let him rub me down with baby oil. It felt so good. I was almost asleep when Stanley's voice startled me as he asked about the bruises on my knees. I quickly made up a lie about mopping and slipping on the tile in my bathroom. He must have believed me because he told me to be more careful as he started kissing my knees.

Sex with Stanley was boring this time. I wasn't into it. My mind was all over the place. I couldn't believe that Mont had run up on me like that. He was going to feel like such an asshole when he found out why Latria and I were in bed together. I didn't know if I was going to ever talk to him again after this stunt.

While I replayed the events of the last few days back and forth in my head, Stanley was giving me oral sex like always. I stopped him before he could get his eight-inch penis into me without a condom. After he put the condom on, I rode him, he rode me, and that was that. After our little sex session, I could barely keep my eyes open. Stanley ordered room service while I took a cool shower to wake myself up. By the time I stepped out of the shower, the food had arrived, and the aroma made my mouth water.

I sat down in the chair wearing one of the plush robes and started to chow down. Stanley watched me as I ate. It was making me feel a bit uncomfortable until he started talking. "So what do you think about me leaving my wife? You never told me."

I replied in a flat voice, "Honestly, I don't think anything. You don't need to leave your wife, and you need to think things over."

Stanley looked worried and said, "Baby, we can do it; we can get a place and start having kids."

I yelled, "Kids? Stanley, do you hear yourself right now? I can't be with you anymore like this. I'm so sorry that it ever went this far. This is wrong, and I'm sorry."

Tears streamed down my cheeks, and I felt sick to my stomach. I didn't want to ruin anybody's marriage. Stanley embraced me and kissed my forehead. He understood that after this, there would be no more us. I took off the robe and got back into my clothes quickly. As I walked down the long hallway, I could feel the distance growing between Stanley and me. We both knew that he needed to be there for his wife. I just hoped and prayed that there was someone out there for me who wasn't married.

On the drive back from the hotel, I cruised with all of the windows down. The fresh air made me feel a lot better and reminded me that I needed to replace Mom's candles. I spotted a candle store in a strip mall not too far from the hotel. I decided to press my luck and see if the store carried Mom's favorite type of candles. As I got out of the car, I looked around and noticed that this strip mall had great shopping potential. Along with the Wax Works Candles and Home accents store that I was going to visit, there was a family-owned sub restaurant, a Marshalls, a Jiffy Lube, and a Target.

I'd gotten only about ten feet away from the car when I heard a horn blow. Startled, I looked back to see what was going on. The horn sounded a lot like Jerry's; lo and behold, it was Jerry. He rolled down the window and yelled my name. I walked over toward his Cadillac, and he pointed at the headlights on my car. I had left them on again. After I turned my lights off, I jogged over to his car and made small talk because it had been a while since we'd seen each other. He told me he missed me and my soft lips. I let out a giggle and lied and told him that we could do something real soon.

Before I left Jerry in the parking lot, he handed me three crisp fifty-dollar bills. I bent down by his car window and kissed his cheek before I left to do my shopping. As I was about to enter the candle store, I saw Jerry's wife coming out with a bunch of bags. I held the door for her so she could make her exit and then went inside to see if the store had Mom's candles.

The money that Jerry gave me brightened up my day. However, finding the exact same candles to replace the ones that Mont and I had broken really took a weight off of my chest. All the way home from the strip mall, I sang along with the radio. As soon as I reached Stone Dale Court, I saw Mom's Land Rover pulled halfway in the garage. My stomach dropped as if I were on a roller coaster. I was ready to see her, but I hoped she didn't ask me about her candles before I could put the new ones where the old ones had been.

19

The New Guy

Over the next couple of weeks, Mom was gone less and less on so-called business trips with Desmond. I didn't have the house to myself like I was used to. Along with Dana, Raquel and Alex had been coming over a lot to keep me company. Mom didn't know what was going on because she was always in her room. I think she and Desmond had stopped messing around, and she was depressed. She wasn't acting like her jolly old self at all.

I did get her out of the house one evening to go to the movies with Alex and me. Before the movie started, Mom insisted that we all go to the restrooms so that we wouldn't have to get up in the middle of the movie. I didn't know why she was treating us like kids, but we did as we were told. Mom went into the ladies' room first, and Alex and I followed not too far behind her.

The face that Mom made when she saw Alex in the ladies' room was priceless. Mom didn't say anything, but it was written all over her face. She had clearly thought Alex was a guy until she saw Alex in the ladies' room. It was funny. I held my laugh in, and I didn't think Alex even noticed Mom gawking at her with her mouth wide open.

After that I could tell Mom thought Alex and I had something going on because she never really left us alone again. When Alex came over, Mom made sure to stay out in the living area or kitchen, so she could see and hear what we were doing. When Alex and I went in my room to get on the computer, Mom kept popping in. She would come in to ask me questions that she already knew the answer to.

It was funny at first, but my mom was starting to get on my nerves. Alex and I ended up hanging out other places, just to get away from my mom. Alex and I got really close, and I considered her one of my best friends. I learned a lot about Alex, and I saw how easy it was for her to pick up girls. If people thought I had drama going on in my life, they should have seen how many chicks Alex was juggling. She was a true player. She had one main girl and four side chicks, and get this: all of the side chicks knew about the main chick, but they didn't know about the other side chicks. The conversations I would listen in on made me laugh out loud. I had to keep a pillow nearby just in case some of the laughter spilled out.

When I wasn't home, I was staying over at Dana's. Her mom didn't even know I was there. All she did was drink stiff drinks and lie out by the pool all day. She didn't have to do anything but wipe her own ass. They had a chef and maids to do all of their dirty work. I wished my mom would go and lie out with Dana's mom. That way she wouldn't be all up in my personal space. The last time Dana had come over, my mom had made sure to bring up Mont. I felt like she knew what was going on between Dana and me. It made me feel really uncomfortable. I knew I had to cut things off with Dana soon.

I never told Mom what had happened between Mont and me. All she knew was that he wasn't coming around anymore. It seemed she really liked him, but if she knew what he had done to me, she would have called some of our guy cousins to come and whip his ass. Mom didn't need to know, so I decided to leave it like that.

One day when I was about to get a little frisky with Dana, my cell phone rang. It was Mom. She had just gotten home from the grocery store and couldn't stop ranting and raving about this guy she'd met. She said his name was Ron, he was Italian, and he resembled John Stamos. And they were going on a date the following weekend. All of that sounded good to me. I told her that I was excited for her and that I would call her back, hurrying to end the call before I moaned in her ear. Dana had been pleasing me with her lizard tongue the whole time I was on the phone, and I was about to explode. That girl just couldn't get enough of me.

Melody was supposed to be coming home soon. I couldn't wait to see her. We had talked on the phone a little, but I still hadn't told her about Dana and me. I was excited to see her reaction. It was cool to talk on the phone, but talking to people in person was different because you got to see their facial expressions. I knew that when I talked to her, I wasn't going to hold anything back; she was getting all of the details. I wondered if she had anything interesting to tell me.

20

Hands On

Thanksgiving, Christmas, and New Year's had come and gone. Melody hadn't made it home for any of the holidays. She was busy studying and working. I hadn't seen her since August, and I was down in the dumps. I spent most of my free time with Dana, Alex, Latria, and Mom. I pampered them all and gave them massages regularly during the winter break. I needed to practice so that my techniques would be on point for the new semester. Dana managed to brighten up my holidays with a gift from her heart. She got me a gold bangle with little hearts engraved all along the inside. I quickly added it to my collection. I couldn't wait to show it off at school.

The first day back to school was going well until my instructor pulled me aside and told me that I couldn't wear my shiny bangles to class during our clinic. Her exact words were "They are quite a distraction." I wanted to act a fool when she gave me the news, which made my blood boil. She did make a lot of sense, though. I knew if I was receiving a massage, I wouldn't want to hear all of that clinking and clanking either. Plus, I wanted to stay on Mrs. Bell's good side, so I nodded my head in consent.

Second semester was going by fast, and I was glad. My grades were looking good. We did a lot of practicing on each other in class, and I got a few pointers from my classmates. I was grateful for the constructive criticism they gave me because it was almost time for clinic to start, the time I had been dreading ever since the first day of class.

Mrs. Bell had us trained like little doggies. We discussed every type of situation that could arise while our client was on the table. Mrs. Bell drilled it in our heads that we always had to keep it professional. I acted like I had it all together, but truthfully, I was a nervous wreck inside.

The Friday before our clinics were set to begin, Mrs. Bell had already sent out e-mails and put flyers on bulletin boards at the local libraries, schools, and professional offices in the community. The appointment book was already filled with clients who had all types of ailments as well as people who just wanted some attention to their aging or overworked bodies. On our way out the door at the end of class, Mrs. Bell gave us the names of our first clients for next week. The guy in front of me had a lady named Mary, and my client's name was Edna.

Saturday was dull. Alex came over, but all she did was use the Internet and talk about her main girl. Latria invited me to church, but I declined and stayed home and watched TV. I couldn't wait to get Monday over with, but the weekend was dragging by. The manager of Island Getaway ended up calling me into work on Sunday around twelve. I accepted the invitation and hoped that I would get some good tips. Work went well. It was really busy, and I managed to stop thinking about Monday.

Mom and Ron were in the kitchen when I got home. The air smelled so sweet. Ron had baked a cake, and they were cleaning up. I went in the kitchen to see if they had a bowl with cake batter still in it that I could eat, but I was a minute too late. I chatted with them for thirty minutes or so and then went upstairs and took a shower. After I ironed my uniform for school, I put my bangles in my jewelry box and shut the lid. That night all I did was toss and turn. I could only think about how tomorrow was going to go.

I felt naked without my bangles. My mind didn't stay on them long, though, because today was the first day of clinic. It went smoothly to my surprise. My client, Mrs. Edna, was a little old lady, and her skin was soft as cotton. Ms. Edna was to receive a full body massage. I gave it my best shot and pretended that I was massaging my granny. I took my time and felt confident after I had completed her massage. After Mrs. Edna put her clothes on, she gave me a big hug and one of those soft peppermints. That had me tickled pink. I was glad that I'd had her for my first client. Mrs. Edna gave me two thumbs up and told Mrs. Bell that she felt like a million bucks.

After my classmates and I completed our first day of clinic, Mrs. Bell praised us for all of the compliments we had received. I was proud and was no longer afraid to give it my all. I felt like my hands could work magic. The next day I had a client named Lance who looked to be about twenty-something. He was really cute, with full lips and neat shoulder-length dreadlocks. Lance was scheduled for a full body massage also.

I was surprised when I learned that he was my client because I was looking for a little old lady again. He shook my hand and beamed his pearly whites at me. I felt my juices starting to flow as I imagined him pleasing me with those full lips. I was brought back to reality when I heard my teacher say that she had to step off campus for a few minutes. Mrs. Bell smiled and said, "I want you to carry on with your clients like the professionals that you are."

I showed Lance to his area so that he could take off his clothes. I gave him little time to undress and quickly reentered the room, hoping that I could sneak a peek at his muscular body. Lance was already lying down on his stomach with the thin blanket over his buns of steel. As I rubbed sanitizer between my palms, I told him that I was going to start the massage shortly. Next, I loaded my hands down with warm oil. I started with his tight shoulders and worked my way down to his ankles and feet. When I asked him to turn over, he asked me if I was sure about that. I replied, "Yes, I'm sure. I have to finish your massage." Lance did as I asked. When he turned over, I noticed a very erect penis; it made the blanket look like a teepee. He kept his eyes closed and had a smile on his fine face.

I tried to stay professional, but Lance's erect penis had all of my attention. My hands yearned to go closer and closer to his groin area. The next thing I knew, I was stroking his manhood. I couldn't believe that I had slipped up. I quickly moved my hands and apologized in a whisper. Lance then lifted his head and whispered, "That needs to be massaged too." Since he had officially given me the go-ahead to fondle his manhood, I continued.

I slid the blanket back and started gently squeezing and stroking him. Then his manhood came to life even more. His penis was a little shorter that Stanley's, but it was much thicker. I really wanted to ride it, but I knew I could never get away with that here at school. So I continued to stroke it until he climaxed, and then I wiped up his love juice with the blanket. Removing the blanket, I smiled and whispered for him to get dressed and told him I would return soon.

Just as I was leaving Lance's room, Mrs. Bell walked by and said, "Lyric, you are doing such a great job. Look at you, taking your linen to the laundry room so soon. I know I'm going to hear good comments about you today!"

I giggled and said, "You sure are, Mrs. Bell." If she only knew what had just happened.

Lance and I ended up exchanging numbers. Before he left, he said, "Do you give massages outside of school?"

I blushed and replied, "Only if the price is right."

21

Weekends Only

On the day that Melody was coming home, I was called in to work at Island Getaway. It was only a four-hour shift, so I declined. I hoped they found someone. Shit, even if they didn't, I wasn't going in. I had already told Dana that I wasn't staying with her this weekend, and she had thrown a big fit. I didn't know what was up with her, but she was becoming clingy, and I didn't like it.

I couldn't wait to see that Maxima roll up this evening. I was thrilled that my mirror image was en route to our home sweet home. Mom, Boogie, and I were waiting on the front porch when Mom noticed that one of the porch lights had blown. As soon as Mom stepped inside to get a light bulb, I saw Melody's car inching closer to our driveway. My heart beat faster and faster as she cut the engine and put her left foot on the ground.

As soon as Melody stood up, I ran from the porch and bum-rushed her. I didn't know who was squeezing who the most. After our long embrace Mom and Boogie finally got a chance to love on Melody. Boogie grabbed most of Melody's luggage out of the backseat, and I grabbed the last bag. I immediately noticed that Melody had all Coach luggage. I knew that had to cost a pretty penny, but I kept that thought to myself.

Mom had made a big breakfast for dinner, so as soon as we got inside, we sat down to eat. I looked over at my sister and saw that she had a brow piercing and blonde highlights in her hair. Mom must have noticed it the same time I did because she belted out, "Melody, what is that mess on your beautiful face?"

Melody replied, "Mom, it's a piercing, and it's not mess. This piercing is bringing attention to my eyes."

Mom laughed and said, "It is kind of cute, but one is enough."

Boogie had to add his two cents too. "It looks freaky," he said. I could have slapped him.

Over cheesy grits, sunny-side-up eggs, sausage links, and homemade biscuits with jam, we caught up. Mom talked about Ron. Melody filled us in on her studies. Boogie talked about how his grades were slipping in college and about this girl he had just met at the mall last week. I talked about the massage clinic and the people who came to our school to get massages. I really enjoyed our meal together. Boogie was being so silly that at times I laughed so hard that I thought orange juice was going to come out of my nose.

After we were done eating, Mom and Melody cleared the table. Boogie and I washed and dried the dishes and put away the leftovers for tomorrow's breakfast. As I was washing the last glass, Boogie whispered to me that J.R. wanted to see Melody, and he wanted it to be a surprise. I smiled and said, "Boogie, I think she's really going to like that." I just hoped that I could keep it a secret. Boogie told me to bring Melody to the pizzeria downtown tomorrow at four so they could be reunited. When we had all of the details sorted out, I turned off the lights in the kitchen and locked the door behind Boogie.

By the time Boogie left, Melody had already taken her bath and was in my bed, yelling for me to come upstairs. I skipped my shower and got in bed with my sister. It was like old times. I told her everything about Alex, Dana, Mont, Latria, and Stanley. She had a million questions, it seemed, and I answered all of them. Melody told me how her roomies had gone from nice and clean to nasty and slack. She said that one of them had begun stealing food and clothes from her and that she'd had enough of them. That's why she'd moved out and gotten herself a condo. I wondered how she could afford all of this by working part-time as a waitress. The wheels in my head were turning rapidly.

When Melody and I were done talking, it was almost two in the morning. I had learned that Melody had two small tattoos, a belly ring, and a nipple ring. I was floored by the new Melody. I didn't know what J.R. was going to think when he saw her tomorrow. Even though we had talked about so much tonight, I still felt like Melody was holding back about something.

The next morning, I woke up to my sister looking directly in my face. It kind of scared me. Before I could say anything, Melody said, "Lyric, there's something else I need to tell you … I dance, but it's only on the weekends."

Wide-eyed, I replied, "What do you mean? Dance like strip?"

Melody put the pillow over her face and whispered, "Yes."

I popped up. I couldn't believe it. That explained the piercing, the tattoos, the condo, and the expensive luggage.

Melody said, "I started off as a bartender, but I became friends fast with one of the most popular dancers at the club. I was making good tips at the bar, but the dancers were really getting paid. They all were driving luxury cars and had really nice condos and townhouses."

Melody then explained how Delight, her voluptuous stripper friend, had given her a few lessons on how to work the pole. I sat back and soaked up everything like a sponge. I didn't know what else to expect from Melody. I was speechless. I couldn't see my sister behaving that way, up on stage grinding and gyrating. This was something I just had to see to believe.

In the middle of this very interesting conversation, the aroma of banana pancakes and bacon made its way up the stairs and into my room, and Mom called us downstairs for breakfast. Melody was surprised to see fresh-cut flowers as a centerpiece and an Italian man wearing a chef's hat while he cooked in the kitchen. Mom immediately introduced Melody to Ron, and she fell in love with him right off the bat. He was such a gentleman, and he had a great sense of humor. I saw the way that he and Mom kept looking at each other. I knew that they had fallen in love already.

After showering I easily could have gone back to sleep, but Melody wanted to go to the spa. I told her that it was all right with me, but I was on a budget.

"Budget?" Melody yelled. She quickly went digging through her bag and pulled out three crumpled one-hundred-dollar bills. She offered me the cash and said, "If this isn't enough, I have plenty more."

I looked at her and said, "Damn, that's your car payment right there, sis. I can't take that."

Melody replied, "Girl, my car is already paid for."

I took the money and held it up to the light to make sure it was real. Melody elbowed me in the ribs and smiled. I wondered if Melody was telling me the whole truth about the stripper story.

22

What Tha

The spa day was much needed. The massages felt different from the ones that I received in class. We both got pedicures, and Melody got a bikini wax. I wasn't down for that just yet. Even though Melody begged me to try it, I still declined. It was almost three o'clock when we left the spa. We weren't meeting up with J.R. and Boogie until four, so I had to kill some more time.

I drove to Screaming Mina's, and Melody hopped out of the car before I could turn off the engine. Within seconds, she was in the window buying stuff off of the mannequins. She bought all kinds of erotic fashions, from fishnet knee-highs to high-heeled shoes; she spent damn near five hundred dollars. All I could do was shake my head because the last time we had come to this store, she had hung out by the exit like she didn't want to be caught dead in here.

Screaming Mina's wasn't far from the pizza spot, so it didn't take long for us to get there when Melody was done shopping. We were seated in a booth near the window. As soon as we started to chat, I saw Boogie and J.R. walking up behind Melody. J.R. was still fine as hell, and I knew Melody was about to flip her lid. When J.R. asked Melody if this seat was taken, she jumped in his arms. They were full of love. The people around us looked and smiled. In the back of my mind, I thought about the abortion and whether she had ever told J.R. about it.

Later that evening, Melody got a suite at a hotel downtown. She said that she wanted to have some fun before she left. I didn't know what Melody had up her sleeve, but I invited a few friends. I told Dana, Alex, and Boogie about it. I was sure they would tell a friend or bring a friend too. When I got to the suite with Dana, whose hands were full of bags, I knocked. Boogie let us into a room of black lights and a strong smell of marijuana. The music sounded exotic, and all we could see were silhouettes bumping and grinding in the dark. I didn't know what the hell was going on, but I was on a mission to find the silhouette that looked close to mine.

When I found Melody, she was dancing on a table in front of J.R. and anybody else who could see. I pulled her down and took her to the bathroom. Her pupils were dilated, and she had a wild look on her face. Her hair looked like she had been riding in a convertible with the top down. I didn't know what drugs my sister had in her system, but she was as high as a kite. I wet a washcloth and tried to wash her face, but it didn't help; she was too far gone. All she was worried about was getting back out there to her man. I couldn't do anything but throw up.

I yelled for Dana to come into the bathroom. When she came in, Melody crawled out on her knees and focused her attention on J.R. He was sitting on the couch, smoking some weed. She hopped on top of him and started humping him like she had just gotten out of jail. My feelings were so hurt that all I could do was cry.

I had never seen my sister like this, and it broke my heart. I cried in Dana's arms until I felt I was ready to go out and try to find some real light bulbs. I needed to see what was going on. When I opened the bathroom door, the music had stopped, and I didn't need any light bulbs to figure it out.

There was a real-life orgy going on right in front of my eyes. Someone had opened the blinds, and the moonlight was telling on everyone. Alex had a girl under the dining room table, Boogie had a plus-size girl up against the wall, and a threesome was going at it on the couch. I was speechless. I didn't see Melody. I hoped that if she and J.R. were having sex, they were at least using a condom. God knows I didn't want to go back to that abortion clinic.

As Dana and I made our way onto the balcony, we saw the two of them in their birthday suits. While J.R. sat in a wicker chair with his head tilted back. Melody was on her knees performing oral sex on him. They didn't even notice that we were standing there. That was the last straw. I had to leave, so Dana drove me home. I knew that my sister had gotten mixed up in the wrong crowd when she started working at that club.

The next day, things were pretty quiet at the house until Melody came in. I was ready to fuss, only I didn't have a chance to because as soon as Melody laid eyes on me, she started apologizing. She got on her knees and asked me to forgive her. Her eyes looked so sad. I asked her how long she had been abusing alcohol and drugs. She told me she had been doing drugs for about three months. Her friend Mark had given her some pills once, and she had been using just about every day since then. I couldn't believe my almost perfect sister was hooked on drugs and alcohol.

23

Busy as a Bee

To keep my mind off of my mirror image and her new bad habits, I stayed busy. I started looking for apartments and hung out with Raquel, Latria, Alex, and Dana. I even went on a date with Lance, the guy from my massage clinic. We had a good time, but I noticed that his breath was a little stinky, and that was an automatic turn-off. When he asked me for a kiss at the end of our date, I thought I would gag. I told him that I didn't kiss on the first date. However, he begged and begged, so I gave him a peck on the cheek just so he would stop talking. As soon as Lance hugged me for the third time, I told him I had to get going. He waved as I backed up out of the parking space. I ended up deleting his number as soon as I got to the stop sign.

The next day, all of my girls were busy, and I was lonely. I called Melody, but I got no answer. I was getting used to her not answering. I left her a message and hoped that she would return my call. I didn't know what made me think about Mont then, but I did. I debated with myself about calling him. I really needed some good loving, but I wasn't sure about him after he'd done me the way he did. I decided to try to hold out. It had been a while since I'd talked to him, and I had been missing him like crazy. Besides, I could play hard for only so long. I decided that the next time he called me, I would answer.

I didn't know what to do with this extra time I had on my hands, so I cleaned out my closet. After I got everything off of the floor and hangers, I made three piles—a throwaway pile, a giveaway pile, and a keep pile. It was ridiculous how much junk I had. As I folded and put away things, I realized how much of this stuff had come from money that guys had given me. I had leather jackets, sweaters, designer jeans, T-shirts, and purses. I couldn't believe how I'd let material things get me to do the very bad things that I had done.

That day I made myself a promise: I was going to try to be a better person. I wasn't going to let a pair of two-hundred-dollar boots pump me up to do something that I knew was morally wrong. I had been raised better than that, and Mom would kill me if she found out about any single thing that I had done. My mind calmed itself as I closed my closet door.

I kicked the piles with my bare feet until they were in the hallway. When I was about to go downstairs and get two trash bags to put the discarded items in, I looked at my room. It wasn't a total pigsty, but it definitely needed to be picked up a little. It took less than thirty minutes to straighten up my room.

I was in such a good mood that I decided to rearrange a few things. When I moved my bed, I found a pair of shoes that I had stopped looking for months ago, three condom wrappers, and a box of letters that my friends had written to me over the years. I decided to tear the letters up and toss them because I was sure that there was incriminating evidence that could get me grounded until the next century. Honestly, I didn't know what had made me think that under the bed was the best place to hide things.

As I moved my bed to the other side of the room, the mattress slipped off the bed a little. When I tried to slide it back into place, I noticed what looked to be a makeup bag tucked underneath the mattress—a Coach makeup bag that matched Melody's luggage. I instantly knew where the bag had come from. I snatched it from under the mattress and looked inside to find over five thousand dollars in one-hundred-dollar bills.

My mouth was dry. I didn't know what to do other than call Melody. I called her and didn't get an answer, so I left a message for her to call me as soon as she could. In the meantime, I put the makeup bag in a boot box on the top shelf in my closet. I figured I would just call her back in an hour or so if she didn't call me first.

After I was done cleaning and rearranging my room, I walked downstairs to get the trash bags for the old clothes. I found Mom and Ron fixing chicken salad and crackers and asked them to fix me a plate too. I went back upstairs to bag up the clothes and zoomed back downstairs so that I could get my plate. I was going to eat at the bar, but Mom and Ron made their way into the living room, so I followed close behind.

An hour later, I was sandwiched between Mom and Ron on the sofa. We were watching a predictable Lifetime movie when the doorbell chimed. The oversized nightshirt I was wearing fell past my knees as I got up. I craned my neck to see the television as I headed for the door. When I looked through the peephole, I thought my eyes were deceiving me, but they weren't. It was Mont. I quickly turned the doorknob and stepped out on the porch. He grabbed me and kissed me. I tried to fight it, but I couldn't resist. He apologized immediately for his behavior. I accepted his heartfelt apology and nodded my head like I was hypnotized.

We sat in his H2 and talked for hours. I told him about Melody. He couldn't believe it. I told him exactly what had happened the night he saw me and Latria in her bed. He felt like an asshole, just like I'd known he would. He didn't even know that her brother had gotten killed. All he could do was shake his head. As we talked, he held my hand and kissed it from time to time. He claimed that he was there to give me the key back to his place, but I wouldn't take it. I told him that we need to start off as friends again and see where that would take us. He agreed.

That night after I got out of the shower, I noticed I had a missed call from Melody. With water still dripping off my wet body, I listened to her message over and over again. With her speech slurred, and the extremely loud background noise, I couldn't make out what she was saying. I attempted to call her back, but she didn't answer. I was so mad that I had missed her call. I could have kicked myself. I didn't sleep well that night; I couldn't stop thinking about Mont and Melody. I went downstairs only to find Mom and Ron asleep on the couch. I quietly made some hot tea and put a little bit of Mom's mango rum in it. That one drink mellowed me out enough that I slept until seven the next morning.

24

Road Trip

Today was the last day of class before spring break. All I wanted to do was have a little fun, but my mind was still on Melody. After class ended, I walked to my car, and decided to call Dana. I told her I was worried about Melody, and she suggested that we go check on her since it was spring break. I was definitely going to take advantage of this weekend off by checking up on my mirror image. I told Mom I was going to visit with Melody for a few days while I packed. She was happy and even insisted that I take some club clothes with me. She had no idea what the underlying reason was for this trip.

We took Dana's BMW, but I drove. I had driven over five hours before I even got in touch with Melody to tell her that we were coming. When she finally answered my call, she sounded totally out of it. I absolutely had to see what was going on and what kind of environment she was in. Two gas stations and three hours later, we pulled into Melody's parking lot. Her condo was really nice on the outside, but we would soon see that the inside was another story.

Melody greeted us at the door with hugs and pointed toward the living room and said, "Excuse the mess. I have been really busy and haven't had time to clean." The condo itself was pretty nice; it kind of reminded me of Mont's place, minus the heated floors and expensive tile in the kitchen and bathrooms. But it looked like it hadn't been cleaned ever. This was not like Melody. She was always neat and clean.

Melody had a three-bedroom condo, but I didn't know that she had a roommate until I heard someone laughing behind a closed door.

"That's Vita, my roommate," Melody said. "I will introduce you to her when she comes out of her room." Melody then showed us to the guest bedroom-and-bath combo, which had only a blow-up mattress, three pillows, a mismatched sheet set, and a mirror leaning against the plain white wall. It was a good thing I had brought my oversized throw blanket from home. Otherwise, Dana and I would have frozen to death. While Melody and I made our way to her room, Dana went outside to get our bags.

Now this was the Melody I knew. Her room was clean as a whistle. It was stylish, painted hot-tamale red with all-white furniture, bedding, and carpet. She took her shoes off as we entered the room, and so did I. Just then, Melody let out a scream and fell back on her bed. I jumped, and she laughed. She told me how glad she was to see me. I then laughed too as I made my way to one of her two closets.

She had a closet for shoes and a closet for clothes. I flipped through all of Melody's stripper attire, and I even tried on a pair of her six-inch heels. I felt like I was walking on stilts. When Dana walked in and saw me in those heels, I thought she would die. She really got a kick out of that.

Melody was acting normal, and I was so happy. After I played dress-up in Melody's shoes, we made our way out to the junky living room. Dana and I pushed some laundry aside on the couch and sat down. Melody talked to us from the kitchen and brought us each a wine cooler. As we drank, Melody told us that she had to work tonight at the club, but she didn't have to dance tonight, just bartend. She asked if we wanted to go, and we declined.

I wanted to have fun, but after all of that driving, I just didn't have the energy. Melody looked pretty bummed out, but I promised her that we would go with her to the club the next night. Melody then ended the conversation and left to take a shower. When she returned, Dana and I lay across her bed and talked to her while she got dressed. Not long after that, Melody was gone.

Late that night, I heard Melody come in. She was fussing and cussing at someone. Then I heard a boom. It sounded like she had tripped over some of the junk in the living room. I wanted to stay awake and be nosy, but my eyelids wouldn't let me. I drifted off into a deep sleep. When I woke up, the sun was barely shining, and Dana was holding me by my waist.

I slowly moved Dana's arm and got up from the air mattress. I wanted to clean this messy house since my sister didn't have time to. I started cleaning the kitchen first, using as much elbow grease as possible. I scrubbed the counters and floors and cleaned out the refrigerator. After I started the dishwasher and hand-washed the dishes that were overflowing out of the sink; I started some breakfast.

Next was the living room. I assumed that the laundry on the couch was clean. I folded the linens, towels, and washcloths and restocked the linen closet. Then I got a trash bag from the kitchen closet and started emptying ashtrays into it. I also trashed empty food wrappers, empty beer and soda cans, and lots of plastic red cups. If I hadn't known better, I would have sworn this was a hangout house.

I spent five minutes looking for a vacuum cleaner that didn't exist. I found the broom and swept until I couldn't sweep anymore. Getting all of the trash onto that flimsy dustpan was a challenge, but the floors sure looked a hell of a lot better.

As soon as I thought I was finished cleaning the living room, I realized that I hadn't fluffed the cushions. They were just as flat as Raquel's butt. I fluffed the pillows, and they actually looked comfortable again. As I placed the pillows back on the couch, I noticed a sock stuck behind the cushion. I assumed it was just a dirty sock until I pulled it out and realized something was in it.

I emptied the sock, and a baggie of pills fell into my dishpan hands. I immediately went to Melody's door and banged on it. She didn't answer. I then tried the doorknob and banged again. As I was pounding on the door, a voice behind me said, "What the hell is going on?"

I turned around, and that was when I met Melody's roommate Vita. She was so confident that all she had on was a neon yellow bra and matching thong. She was just as dark as Stanley's wife, but her skin was flawless. She also had full lips and hips, a huge shapely ass, and a delicate six-pack. If Vita wore a jogging suit outside, she could stop traffic. That's how bad her body was.

While I was checking her out, I secretly stuffed the sock into my pajama pocket. I introduced myself, and Vita totally brushed me off. Apparently, she was upset because I'd woken her from her beauty rest, which she didn't need.

The scowl on Vita's face disappeared when she noticed that the house was clean. She gave me a faint "nice to meet you" and sat her bare ass on the couch. She then stretched for the remote control and put her perfect cotton-candy-pink toes on the spotless glass coffee table. As I headed down the hall to clean the bathroom, Vita asked what that smell was. I told her that I had some cheese grits on the stove and bacon in the oven.

She frowned and said, "I don't eat pork or cheese."

"Well, I guess you won't be eating breakfast with us then," I said. "What a pity."

Vita sucked her teeth. Then she went back in her bedroom and slammed the door so hard that the wall shook. I was glad she left because I was ready to give Vita a knuckle sandwich for breakfast. I was sick of this girl, and I had just met her ill ass.

I went to the bathroom and closed the door. I pulled the pills out to examine them a little more closely. They were different colors with little hearts and stars on them. I knew that these pills were illegal drugs, and I knew Melody was using them. I thought I had seen a few on her nightstand in her room the day before, but I wasn't 100 percent sure. They might have been vitamins or something.

I flushed the socks, baggie, and pills right down the toilet. I then cleaned the bathroom with bleach and had to open a window because I used too much. I had to get all of those nasty germs out of there. I flushed the toilet one last time before I left the bathroom.

25

The Last Straw

That night Melody was super excited about Dana and me going to see her on stage for the first time. I was more than a little nervous. Since I had packed only boring clothes, Melody insisted that I wear something of hers. I decided to wear a pair of tight white jeans and a hot-pink belly shirt. Dana, of course, had on a polo. Melody had a bag packed with a fishnet bodysuit and a see-through glittery outfit. I couldn't believe that I was going to see Melody strut her stuff tonight.

When we entered the club, "Hypnotized" by Plies was playing. Melody led Dana and me to the bartender and introduced her to us as Sugar. I waved at Sugar, and she winked at me. Melody then told Sugar to take care of us. That was music to my ears. Just then, I heard the dee-jay introduce the next dancer. It was Vita. I rolled my eyes as the guys ran from the bar and up to the stage.

Melody ordered all of us a shot, and we took it to the head. My throat was on fire. Melody then asked Sugar for a "one hitter quitter." I didn't know what that was, but Sugar poured a whole lot of liquor into a plastic cup and then put an orange pill in Melody's drink as she handed it to her. Melody drank it down in a flash and was off to get dressed.

The pill that Sugar had put in Melody's drink looked a lot like the pills I had flushed this morning. I was going to say something to Melody, but she ran off too fast. I looked at Dana and shook my head. Not too long after that, Sugar pointed Dana me I to a reserved table. I was feeling good. The music was pumping, and the drinks were flowing. I was giving Dana a lap dance when I saw a crowd coming our way.

It was platinum rapper Know Betta and his entourage. They had big-booty girls with weaves down to their asses and muscle men wearing extra small tank tops. I couldn't believe it. This was one of Mont's favorite rappers. When Know Betta and his clan made it to the VIP section, the velvet rope was put up and the muscle men stood by it, flexing their muscles.

Just as the club settled down, the deejay introduced Melody. She was wearing a white fishnet bodysuit with clear seven-inch platform heels. The song that she slid down the pole and popped her booty to was one of Know Betta's greatest club hits. The guys were going crazy. Even rapper Know Betta was at the stage, throwing ridiculous amounts of cash. It was really raining dollar bills, and all of them were for my mirror image.

I was in awe. Melody was climbing poles and dropping down in splits. I couldn't believe my sister could do all of that. At the end of Melody's act, Know Betta whispered something in her ear, and she blushed. She then shook her head and helped a bouncer gather her hard-earned money. One bouncer was shoving Melody's money into a five-gallon bucket; another bouncer was on the side, sweeping up money. I had seen it all tonight.

When Melody returned to the floor, she was wearing the glittery see-through outfit. She was trying her best to make it through the crowd, but guys kept flagging her down with money and requesting lap dances.

It was thirty minutes later before Melody reached our table. I hugged her and told her she had done great. She beamed with happiness. When Melody leaned in to tell me that she had just made over two thousand dollars, I noticed that her speech was slurred. It sounded like it had the other day when I talked to her on the phone.

Just as I was about to pull Melody outside to talk to her about her roommate and the pills I had found this morning, one of the muscle men from Know Betta's entourage tapped her on the shoulder. The guy with the muscles pointed toward Know Betta in the VIP section, and Melody giggled and walked off with Mr. Muscle Mania. She looked over her shoulder and yelled, "Don't wait up!"

As much as I wanted to chase Melody, I decided this wasn't the right time. I blew her a kiss, and she caught it. I watched Melody as she made it past the velvet rope. She sat on Know Betta's lap, and as he spoke, I read his lips: "Damn, you smell good." I shook my head and decided to stop stalking my sister. I turned my attention to Dana and bought both her and myself a lap dance.

We left the club and returned to Melody's condo around two in the morning, only to be welcomed back to a full-blown house party. The music was bumping, and the smoke was so thick it looked like smog. I could have sworn we were in Los Angeles instead of Atlanta. There were people everywhere, and the house was completely trashed. The cleaning I had done this morning had been pointless. You couldn't even tell that I'd done anything. This had me pissed. I found the stereo and snatched the plug out of the wall.

With the music off, there was total silence for a moment. All I heard was someone throwing up in the freshly cleaned bathroom that I had scrubbed this morning. A few people started complaining. One person shouted, "What happened to the damn music?" I noticed there were pills on the coffee table, right where Vita was sitting. As I approached Vita, I told her that she needed to get these people out of here.

She said with a smirk, "Bitch, why you turn the music off? You don't run shit around here. Ain't nobody going nowhere!"

As Vita got up and headed toward the stereo to plug it back in, she brushed up against me. Before I knew it, I had snatched Vita, and my bangles sounded like a tambourine falling down a flight of stairs. Vita got one good punch in, and then I went after her ass like I was getting paid to fight. I was beating her real good before Dana and some guy broke us up. I didn't know if she just couldn't fight or if she just couldn't function because she was on those damn pills.

Either way, I was still angry about the house being messed up. Dana dragged me into the guest bedroom and finally got me to calm down. I ran straight to the mirror to see if there was any damage to my face. I had a busted lip, but that was it. I could still hear Vita out there, talking shit. I knew she didn't want me to come back out there.

My blood was still boiling when I dialed Melody's cell. It just rang and rang. I called my mirror image twelve times before I concluded that she wasn't going to answer. I figured she was still with Know Betta and his crew. I left her a message telling her about the party and the fight.

My head was thumping just as loud as the music was. Someone had plugged the stereo back in. I went to the bathroom, put the lid down, and sat on the toilet. Dana wet a washcloth and wiped my face with it. She then ran a bath with lots of hot, steamy water. After we soaked and relaxed, we had sex. Not long after that, the party settled down, and it was finally quiet.

26

The Truth Hurts

I was roused from my sleep by arguing and booming sounds. When I realized that one of the voices arguing was Melody's, I yanked the bedroom door open and found Melody and Vita going at it like a cat and a dog. I assumed they were fighting over the party and the fight from last night until I heard Melody say something about a sock full of pills. As much as I wanted to help Melody beat down Vita some more, I didn't. I broke up the two of them and almost broke my neck in the process by tripping over the couch cushions that were scattered all over the floor.

As soon as Vita was free from Melody's death grip, she ran to her room with her almost-ripped-out weave and a bloody nose. I knew that there was going to be a big door slam after that, and there was. Melody's eyes were bloodshot, and she was breathing like she had just run a marathon. I knew it was time to tell her about finding and flushing the sock.

I told Melody that Vita hadn't stolen her pills, and Melody asked how I knew that. I explained to her that I had found them stuck in the couch when I was cleaning and that I had tried to wake her up to ask her about them, but she never opened the door for me. So I flushed them.

Melody yelled, "What the hell do you mean, you flushed the sock?"

Before I knew what hit me, I felt fire on the left side of my face. Melody had slapped the taste out of my mouth. I was speechless. I held my face as I watched my drug-fiend mirror image run to the bathroom and stick the same hand that she had slapped me with down the toilet. I stood at the bathroom door and watched in disbelief as Melody got the plunger and started pumping the toilet. I could tell that she was praying silently to herself that the toilet would regurgitate the sock, baggie, and pills.

Needless to say, the pills didn't appear. They were long gone. Even though I was disgusted by Melody's behavior, I pulled her away from the toilet and embraced her, nasty toilet hand and all. I then led Melody through the junky living room and straight to her bedroom.

That Sunday morning, Melody let all of the skeletons out of her closet. I asked her about the money she had left under my mattress, and she told me that she wanted me to keep it, just in case something happened to her. I didn't quite understand why Melody would say something like that until she told me about the lifestyle she had been living since moving to Atlanta.

Tears pooled at the corners of my eyes as she told me that she had dropped out of school and had been drinking a lot. Melody then admitted to selling ecstasy and prescription pain pills to the dancers at most of the strip clubs in the area for this guy named Mark. The first night Melody met Mark, all of the girls were all over him, but he was interested only in her. Their friendship started with them just hanging out at the club, but when he asked her to go home with him one night, she fell into his trap.

Within the next few weeks, Mark had Melody selling drugs and influencing girls at the club to sleep with men for money. Melody was Mark's top girl until she decided to leave Mark and pimp herself out. Before Melody cut Mark off completely, she had a chance to sex one of Mark's suppliers, and since then, she had been getting the drugs from him. She had made a lot of cash and had a safe in her closet full of money to prove it.

After hearing all about Melody's drinking and drug problems, I couldn't think straight. Plus, my face was still sore as ever from that slap. I heard someone in the living room moving around; I assumed it was Dana. Another hour of talking with Melody made my mouth dry. I asked Melody if she wanted something to drink, and she said sure. When I opened the bedroom door, the living room was spotless once again, only this time Vita had cleaned it up.

She had what was left of her weave tied up and had on some boy shorts with a spaghetti-strap tank top. I didn't say anything to her as I crossed the living room to go back into the guest bedroom. Dana was just waking up. I cuddled with her for a few minutes before I told her about the fight. She couldn't believe that she had slept through it.

Before I left Sunday afternoon, Melody gave me half of the money from her safe. I didn't feel comfortable driving with such a large amount of cash, but she begged me to take the money, so I did. Melody promised that she would get help with her drinking and drug problem as we hugged and kissed each other good-bye. I promised that her secret would stay between her and me. A part of me wanted to stay with her a few more days. I wanted to watch over her to make sure that she kept her promise. But I knew I couldn't stay. Even though it was spring break, I had to go back to work tomorrow.

As the weeks went by, I talked to Melody less and less. When I called her, she always had to get off the phone in a hurry. One time she tried to hang up so fast that she didn't press the button right to end the call.

I listened to some guy boss her and another girl named Crystal around. The guy was belting out orders like they were slaves. I had a bad feeling that this guy was a pimp, and Melody was one of his top girls.

After hearing what I heard on the phone, I knew that Melody was still hooked on drugs and that she had broken her promise to me. I wondered if she had even gotten back into school. I had been thinking too much, and I had to talk to someone. So I decided to pay Latria a visit.

I told Latria about Melody and her drug habit. Since Melody had broken her promise to me, I felt like I could break mine too. I felt a little weight lift off of my shoulders after talking with Latria. But after that day, I didn't talk to Melody for a while because she wouldn't answer her phone. She did call me late one night with music bumping in the background, but I could barely understand her. All I could make out was that she had made over three thousand bucks in one night. She said that she was going to send me some money, but I never received it.

The next week I called Melody multiple times, but she never answered. I left her message after message and heard nothing back at all. I was so desperate to talk to her that I decided to call the club and see if she was there. The young girl who answered the phone was giggling when she picked it up. She said that she hadn't seen Melody as often as usual and that she had been missing her shifts quite often the past couple of weeks. When I heard this, my mind started racing. I didn't know how to handle this. I was scared, but I knew I had to tell Mom if I didn't hear from Melody by the end of the weekend.

Sunday came and was almost over, and I still hadn't heard anything from Melody. I now knew that it was time to let the cat out of the bag. I didn't know how my mom was going to take it, and I didn't know how to tell her. I decided to call Latria and get some advice. She told me to just let things flow naturally with my mom, so that's what I did. I casually went into Mom's room and sat on the foot of her bed. She was folding some laundry and watching TV.

I started the conversation by asking Mom when she had last heard from Melody. Just then, the phone rang, and whoever it was had Mom's full attention. "Yes, this is," she said. "Yes ... yes." The next thing I knew, Mom was screaming, and laundry was all over the place. I tried to ask Mom what was wrong, but I immediately knew when she yelled, "No, not my baby! Why, God, why?"

My blood instantly ran ice-cold.

27

Dehydrated

My heart was broken. No, it was stolen—snatched right out of my chest and put into a blender set on pulverize. I had never hurt like this before. I was a basket case. I couldn't control my emotions. I wanted to die. I wanted to be with her. I didn't want to look in another mirror again. I was afraid to face myself. This was my fault. I should have said something to Mom about Melody's problem as soon as she told me.

I had never cried so much in my life. My eyes were bloodshot. I tried pulling my hair out, kicking, screaming, and throwing up. But it didn't matter what I did. Melody was dead from an accidental drug overdose at the tender age of twenty. The coroner wanted to rule that it was a suicide, but Mom wouldn't let him. She said that Melody had way to much going for herself and that she wouldn't have committed suicide. This absolutely did not seem real.

The last time anyone had seen Melody was about three o'clock Saturday morning. Melody had worked at the club Friday night and was supposed to be the first one on the stage Saturday, but she never showed up. Delight, a stripper at the club, called Melody several times, but she never got an answer. She decided to go to Melody's condo to see if she was home. After she had knocked on the door for five minutes or so, grumpy, pill-popping Vita let her in. Delight explained that she couldn't get in touch with Melody, and Vita told her that she had seen Melody stumble into her bedroom earlier and close the door. After they came to the conclusion that Melody might still be in her bedroom, they tried to get in, but they were unsuccessful.

Neither of them knew what to do, so they contacted the property manager and got him to unlock Melody's bedroom door. That's when Vita, Delight, and the property manager discovered Melody unresponsive in her bed, still in the black catsuit that she had left the club wearing. From there they called 911, and the ambulance came to pick up Melody, only to announce her DOA. It took them a few hours to notify the family.

Melody died on a Saturday, and we ended up having the funeral on a Saturday because of some family members who couldn't find earlier flights. I would hate Saturdays from now on, and I questioned whether I wanted to live anymore because I could have told Mom earlier, and she could have gotten Melody the help that she needed. The funeral was held at our old high school gymnasium. The turnout was huge. Mom and Dad picked out a beautiful iridescent casket with silver accents. Melody looked so beautiful in it. I picked out her clothes for the funeral. I chose a teal dress and a cream lace blazer. I held up pretty well at the beginning of the funeral, but when it was time to view the body for the last time, I totally lost it. I ended up fainting.

When I came to, I heard sirens. Boogie and his mom were kneeling over me and fanning me with one of the programs from Melody's service. I was laid out on the floor of the gymnasium, and everyone else was gone. I immediately jumped up and ran outside, but I had missed the family car to the cemetery. The medics checked me out, and I was okay. But by the time Boogie, his mom, and I made it to the grave site, Melody's casket was in the ground, and the men had already started shoveling the dirt on top of it. I was horrified.

Back at the house, cars were lined up just like they had been for our graduation. I went right to my room and got in the bed with my heels and everything on. My bangles jingled a sad tune as I pulled the covers over my head. I cried and cried. No one could soothe me. Mom tried. Dad tried. Raven tried.

That night was horrible; I couldn't sleep because I kept thinking of Melody cold and all alone in that beautiful casket. I kept visualizing her lying there. Even though most of the family was still at the house, I slept with Mom, and Ron slept on the couch. My pillow was soaked. Mom rubbed my back and tried to soothe me, but reality had set in, and I just couldn't take it.

The next morning we had a big breakfast at our house before Dad and the rest of our family members flew back to their homes. I attended even though I had a headache from out of this world. Most everyone was in good spirits. Mom had invited Dana and Latria over to see if they could cheer me up, but it didn't work. All I did was lie around and sulk. I didn't know how or if I was ever going to get over this.

Boogie's mom made me some homemade brownies and sent them over when he and J.R. came to visit me. Mom and Ron had gone to the gym, so it was just us three, and it was quiet in the house. When J.R. blurted out, "I wish she would have had our baby," my nerves had me so messed up that I threw up right where I stood. While J.R. stood there crying, Boogie ran into the downstairs bathroom to get a towel and some tissue. My body felt hot and weak as I watched Boogie try to calm J.R. down.

Boogie finally had to call his mom to come get J.R. He had totally lost it. As he left, he apologized to me and told me that he would have been a great father. I couldn't even look at him. Tears ran down my face as I dropped to my knees in the vomit. I yelled at the top of my lungs, "I wished Melody would have had the baby too! Maybe then she wouldn't have gone to that stupid college and got mixed up with those no-good so-called friends of hers."

Boogie managed to calm me down, and he even got me clean clothes from my closet to put on. After he cleaned the carpet where I had vomited, he put the stinky towels and my clothes in the washing machine. I sat on the couch and stared into space as he turned on the television and went to the kitchen and got the tray of his mother's brownies. As he started to eat, my head fell on his shoulder, and I drifted off into a much-needed slumber with the wonderful aroma of the brownies dancing in my nostrils.

28

Hurts So Bad

As the days turned into weeks, I adjusted little by little. After graduating from College with a certificate in applied science, I started a job at the spa Melody had gotten her bikini wax at. I found a one-bedroom apartment about fifteen miles from Stone Dale Court. It wasn't anything fancy, but I knew I could make it cozy with some pillows, pictures, mirrors, and curtains. Mom, Boogie, and Ron helped me move in. I didn't really have a lot, which was fine. I had a few pieces of furniture from Mom's house, and Boogie's mom gave me a nice love seat and a recliner. It fit my small space perfectly.

My bedroom was a good size. It had a closet that was about the same size as the one back at Mom's house. I had enough space for my old full-size bed, a nightstand, and a dresser. I ended up bringing all of my clothes and two small boxes of Melody's stuff too. I had a hall closet, which I made into a shrine for Melody. It had some of her certificates, novels with broken spines, her favorite T-shirts, her nerd glasses, and pictures. Everything was placed in its own special space. I opened the closet on a daily basis and sat and talked to Melody like she was right there. At that time it was just what I needed to give me peace of mind.

I hit "play" on my life during the week, but I was on pause on the weekends. I worked Monday through Friday. I wore the same boring navy and coral scrubs every day. I massaged the same tired feet, aching backs, and stiff necks. I was exhausted mentally. I was the one who needed a damn massage. If only I could massage myself. I had offers, but I didn't want anybody touching me at the moment. If I wasn't at work, I was shut up in my apartment like a hermit crab, just me and Melody's shrine. That was just the way I liked it.

One day when I got home, there were a dozen pink roses sitting outside my door. I immediately thought they were from Mont, but I was wrong. They were from Dana. The card simply said, "Call me." Mom must have told her where I was staying. She had been calling me like crazy, but I hadn't been picking up the phone for anybody except Mom and Raven. The roses reminded me of Melody's funeral, so I just left them outside the door.

Later that night, I opened the exterior door of my apartment, and the roses were still sitting there. I brought them inside and set them in the middle of the coffee table. I had to admit, the flowers made me feel better, and they gave off a nice aroma. I sent Dana a text message that read, "Thank you." Her response was a smiley face and a heart. I smiled to myself as I sat cross-legged in front of the closet and looked at all of Melody's things.

For dinner I ate Melody's favorite variety of Oodle Noodles and started reading a book that I had taken from her room and put in the closet. The book was great. I couldn't put it down. I now understood why she was always reading. Her book took me to a whole new world. I read throughout the night and was finished with the book by dawn. I fell asleep for almost two hours before it was time to get ready for work.

When I arrived at work, I learned that I was scheduled for a nine-ty-minute massage that hadn't been in my appointment book the day before. I really didn't feel like getting to know any new clients, but since I was already there, I figured that I might as well work and make the money. I started getting the massage room ready for my new client. As I turned down the lights and pressed play on the CD player, my walk-ie-talkie sounded, and the receptionist notified me that my client was at the front desk. I quickly made my way toward the front of the spa to introduce myself to the client, but I stopped short when I saw who it was.

After a split second, I continued to the front desk and introduced myself as if I didn't know him. When we reached the massage room, I closed the door and whispered, "What are you doing here?"

Jerry whispered back, "To get some attention from you since you never return any of my calls."

I sighed, Jerry opened his arms, and I gave him a big hug. He told me that he had heard about my sister, and he insisted that he had been calling to see if I was okay, not to hook up or be frisky.

I gave Jerry a kiss, and his beard tickled my face. I knew that he cared about me a lot, and I felt bad for blowing him off after seeing him at the shopping plaza that day. My thoughts subsided when he put his index finger on my lips and told me to relax, get undressed, and lie down on the massage table facedown. I did as I was told. He maneuvered his lean body around the room, pumped hot oil into his hands, and started massaging my neck.

He worked his way down to my shoulders, lower back, and legs. I was drooling out of the side of my mouth by the time he made his way down to my ankles and feet. I secretly thanked God for Jerry coming here today. I had really needed this. It had been so long since someone had touched me and not wanted sex. After my massage was over, Jerry told me to get dressed. As I was putting on my clothes, Jerry made a small pallet on the floor with the thin sheets and heated blankets from the massage table.

We lay on the floor, and he held me. We didn't talk; we simply lay there. I appreciated him for this. When we had only about ten minutes left in the ninety-minute massage session, Jerry helped me clean the room and set it up for my next client. Before he left, he gave me a sixty-dollar tip and asked me to please answer the next time he called me. I nodded, and he kissed me on my forehead before leaving the room.

The day was a blur after Jerry left. I kept checking my phone to see if he had called or sent me a text message, but he hadn't. On my lunch break Mom called and invited me to dinner, and I agreed to show up. I had three more massages scheduled for the day, and after that, I was done. I was ready to see what Mom or Ron had cooked. I planned to try to eat a little, and then I was going home to my cozy little apartment to soak in a hot bubble bath.

29

Life Goes On

One year had passed since Melody's death. My heart was still broken, and I felt empty inside. I didn't think that I'd smiled since the last time I talked to her. I had taken down all of the mirrors in my apartment because I didn't want to be reminded of her. Whenever I saw my reflection, I felt like it was her looking at me, asking why I hadn't told Mom that she was in too deep and needed help. Honestly, I had thought about killing myself, but I knew that Mom, Dad, Raven, and Ron wouldn't know what to do.

I hadn't had sex in over a year, and I was okay with that. I guess I was celibate. I still hadn't been eating much either. I'd lost about twenty pounds since the day I found out that my mirror image had left me. I had never looked so small and disheveled in my life.

My hair was a mess, full of split ends, uneven, and badly broken off. My nails were bitten down to the quick, and my face was so broken out that even Proactiv didn't help. I didn't look like myself anymore. I didn't know who I was anymore.

The only person I had really been talking to was Jerry. He had been keeping me borderline sane, but I couldn't talk to him often because his wife had gotten hurt at work and was home all the time. One day, I finally broke down and decided to answer the phone for Latria, who had been calling me every day. The first question she asked me was whether I felt like having company. I didn't, but I told her that she could come by because I felt like I was about to go crazy.

Within the next thirty minutes, I heard her coming up the stairs to my apartment. I opened the door as she reached the top step and lunged out for her. She gave me the biggest hug, and I felt like butter in a frying pan. I melted into her arms, and we cried together. Since we were both twins, and we'd both had to bury our mirror images, we really had more in common than what we used to. I finally understood that she needed this just as much as I did. Answering the phone for Latria that day was the best thing that I could have done.

The following week, I answered calls from anyone who rang my phone. It was good to talk with my old friends. Alex was still having drama with all of her girlfriends, and the situations that she had been getting herself into almost made me split my side from laughter. I had to admit, I wasn't as down in the dumps as I had been. Raquel even brought her baby boy over for me to see. He was so cute. He was definitely going to be a heartbreaker.

Dana invited me to lunch, and I accepted her invitation. When I got in her car, she just looked at me with her eyebrows scrunched up. I looked torn up from the floor up.

We went to lunch like she had suggested and then to the salon near the mall. I ended up having to get three inches of my hair cut off. I wasn't happy about that, but at least now I looked like somebody who gave a damn. I let the nail technician give me a manicure with what little nails I had left. I chose an iridescent color that just so happened to be the color of Melody's casket.

As the weeks continued to fly by, I picked up a few pounds and started wearing makeup again. I was feeling okay about life, but I missed my sister like crazy. I decided that it was time for me to visit Melody's grave at the cemetery. The weather was a bit gloomy, but I made up my mind that today was the day. Rain or shine, I was going to that cemetery.

I parked and got out with a dozen pink tulips. There was a peaceful wind blowing. I took a deep breath and walked as slowly as I could until I reached Melody's grave. I put the tulips on the top of her headstone and sat cross-legged on the damp grass. I ran my hands across the lettering and the picture of her. Then the tears and snot came. I talked and talked to her, snorting and crying, until I had a headache. Before I stood up, I leaned over and hugged the tombstone.

When I got back to my apartment, Latria was there waiting. I had told her that I was going to the cemetery, and she wanted to be there for me when I got back. I felt like a weight had been lifted off of my shoulders. All of that crying and talking really had done me some good. Later that evening, Latria and I looked at old pictures of my family. There were so many pictures of me and Melody dressed alike that it was ridiculous.

I asked Latria if she would help me hang the mirrors back up, and she nodded yes. Five mirrors and two cups of hot tea later, Latria decided that it was time for her to get back to her side of town. We hugged and wished each other a good night. She told me that she was proud of me as she left. As soon as she had driven off in her new Malibu, I went to the full-length mirror in my closet, stood, and looked at myself for several minutes before I kissed the mirror and said good night to Melody.

Two months later, I still hadn't had any contact with Stanley, but he kept putting money in my bank account. Every time I went to check my balance, it always had an extra few hundred dollars or so in it. I did see him and his wife at the mall one day, but he didn't see me. They looked happy, holding hands and everything. Stanley was carrying all of the bags, and he was wearing the same loafers like always. I ducked inside a store and watched them make their exit, and then I went the opposite way and continued to window-shop. Honestly, I hadn't been thinking about him. After that day at the hotel, I had put all of that behind me, and I hadn't looked back.

Mont had been there for me, I had to admit. He was calling and checking up on me like we were back together, but we weren't. He had left a box on my doorstep shortly after the funeral. It had a single bangle in it, engraved with the words "Lyric's Melody," and that was it—no card, note, or anything. I was going to call and tell him thank you, but he knew I was thankful.

Deep down I wished Mont wouldn't have cheated and flipped out on me like he did. I would have loved being back in a serious relationship with him, but I had lost all my trust in him when he cheated on me. I did miss that chocolaty man, and when I thought about his large blessing, it made me bite my bottom lip.

As for Dana and me, we took a chill pill and got back to normal. Things had been getting a bit out of hand. She had been getting jealous and wanted me to stay every night with her. I couldn't deal with that, plus my mom wouldn't approve of that type of lifestyle. I had to get myself out of that situation before things became obvious. Dana and I still talked from time to time, and she still gave me the hookup on underclothes. She had a new chick now; she wasn't as cute as me, though. Dana told me that she couldn't be happier, but I suspected that she just wanted me to feel jealous.

Mom was taking it day by day; she had her moments about Melody just like I did. She finally confessed that she and Desmond had been in a relationship, but she had let it go because she knew it wasn't right. Mom left DO TELL advertising company and didn't look back. She and Ron were engaged now and just opened a catering business of their own. Coco's Creations had better watch out because Ron and Mom could throw down in the kitchen.

Latria and I grew closer, and I came to consider her my best friend, even though we'd met under some pretty messed-up circumstances. She still worked at the DMV, and she told me all kinds of stories about the jerks who came through her line. One day she told me that she'd met a nice guy at her gym, and she wanted me to meet him and his brother. So I agreed that we might go on a double date sometime within the next few weeks. *Who knows?* I thought. Maybe this would be the guy who would help me settle down and get rid of all these bangles from my broken past.

Made in the USA
Middletown, DE
24 September 2016